My Mom's a Mortician

Kevin Kirk Chronicles

Cover illustration © J. M. Quinn

Published by Covenant Communications, Inc.
American Fork, Utah

Printed in Canada
First Printing: May 2004

12 11 10 09 08 07 06 05 04   10 9 8 7 6 5 4 3 2 1

ISBN 1-59156-433-6

My Mom's a Mortician

Kevin Kirk Chronicles

a novel by Patricia Wiles

This book is dedicated to
Terrie Bittner, for her enCOURAGEment;
to David Woolley, for his persistence; and to
"The Wise Old Man of the Lake," Herbert J. Cox,
for teaching my son how to fish.

Chapter One

Mom's secret tomato-and-green-peppers-recipe meat loaf always made me sick. It had even more gag power the night she announced we were moving two hundred miles away to some boring Arkansas delta town to run a funeral home.

I'd worked hard at showing no interest in Mom's new career as a mortician. Maybe that's why my parents didn't discuss the move with me earlier. I was good at ignoring their conversations about mortuary science. And thanks to my Game Boy and earphones, I didn't hear a word of Mom's graduation ceremony the night before.

Now I wished I'd paid attention.

It was bad enough that my friends knew Mom was going to school to be an undertaker. But at least we lived where I had friends.

Now I had to move where I had no friends at all: Armadillo, the roadkill capital of Arkansas. Population 7,836—give or take a few decaying marsupials.

It was too late for discussion. They'd already bought the place and signed the deal. But no one thought to ask me how I felt about it.

For some strange reason, my parents thought I should be happy about this.

I spit an unchewed mouthful of meatloaf into my napkin. "Just a minute," I said, "if you two want a funeral home, that's fine. But you're not gonna drag me into the dead body business!"

Dad yanked the napkin out of my hand and tossed it in the trash. "Do you know what the price of ground beef is these days?" He had no sympathy for my discomforts, whether caused by Mom's inability to cook a dead cow or her ability to embalm one. "Look, Kevin, morticians provide an important service. It'll be a different lifestyle. It's not an eight-to-five job. But we'll get used to it. We've adjusted to Mom's school schedule over these last two years, and we've made it OK."

"But Dad—"

"We're going to pay you," Mom interrupted. Dad gave her a puzzled look—a clue that Mom's bribe was a spur-of-the-moment attempt to soften me up. He had to be wondering where Mom thought the money would come from. He hadn't been able to find a steady job since the factory shut down. He'd insisted that Mom stay in school instead of looking for work. While Mom studied, we scraped by on savings plus whatever handyman jobs Dad could find. I'd even mowed grass, raked leaves, and shoveled snow to help pay the bills.

I should have questioned why she was willing to pay me. But I needed a new bike, and despite my misgivings, the promise of money was hard to resist. "How much?"

Dad could see I'd taken the bait. So instead of arguing with Mom, he reeled me in. "It depends on how business goes at first. You'll start at a smaller amount, of course, but as the business grows, we'll be able to pay you more." Then he twirled the corner of his moustache, and in his best Dracula accent he said, "And I promize zat you shall never, ever haf to touch zee corpses."

Mom pulled a brochure out of her three-ring binder and tossed it across the table. On the front of the brochure it said: "Paramount Funeral Home, serving Sherman and White Counties since 1959." Inside was a photograph of a two-story brick building with tall, white columns. I covered the long black hearse with my hand, and tried to convince myself that my parents were going to manage a country club instead of a funeral home.

Mom then tore a packing list out of the binder and handed it to me. "We'll open at the end of July, so we have less than six weeks to get ready. It'll take four weeks to get the home presentable, which leaves only two weeks for the move. So tomorrow I'll go to Food-a-Rama and get some empty boxes . . ." Her tongue clicked like an out-of-control metronome as she checked her mental list. "We'll work through the bedrooms first. Then I'll start in the den. We'll tackle the kitchen last. There's so much to organize!"

She grabbed the first issue of her new subscription to *Mortician's Monthly* and left the table for a long soak in a hot bath. I flopped down on the couch and turned on the TV, figuring if Dad thought worm food was so great he could clean up the leftovers of Mom's meat loaf without me.

The next day, the first morning of summer break, Mom pitched two produce boxes and one of those fake apple-juice-drink pouches through my bedroom door. The juice pouch sailed across the room and hit me in the shoulder. I rolled over on my back and groaned.

"Eat fast, Kev! Gotta pack," she yelled, using my forehead as a target for a package of apple-raspberry Toaster Tarts. I sat up in bed and rubbed my eyes.

Dad was under my desk, disconnecting my computer. "Honey, bring me something to wrap around this monitor . . . a blanket or something." Then he sneezed three times. "For cryin' out loud, Kevin. Don't you know how to use a vacuum? There are dust balls under here big enough to shoot hoops with. Honey, bring up a couple more boxes."

Mom brought in three more boxes and some old blankets. She dumped them on the floor beside Dad. It surprised her that I was still in bed.

"Kevin Andrew Kirk, get out of that bed right now! There's work to do." She jerked the sheets off the bed, sending my Toaster Tarts flying through the air. They hit the wall above my computer desk and fell behind it.

Dad was losing patience with the endless yards of printer and power cables. "Freda, where are my boxes? Kevin, stop throwing your food." He tried to pitch the tarts on the bed, but his direction was off. They veered toward Mom and landed at her feet. She picked them up and put them on my bed.

No one seemed to care that my breakfast had been knocked around the room like the volleyballs in PE class. "How am I supposed to eat those Toaster Tarts?" I knocked them off the bed and brushed the crumbs off my mattress. "They're beat up and covered in dust bunnies."

Mom wadded my sheets into a tight bunch. She looked at Dad's rear end sticking out from under my desk, and then she looked at me. I stuck my bottom lip out in a pout. I didn't want to pack. It was the first day of summer. And I was hungry.

Mom threw the sheets down and left the room again. When she came back, she handed me a new package of tarts. She didn't say anything. She didn't even smile. She just stuck the tarts out and shook them in front of my face. I knew then I'd pushed my limit. I took the tarts and even said thanks, but it was too late. I'd gone too far. The puddles in her eyes let me know she was frustrated. I decided it was time to get up, get dressed, and start packing.

By the end of the day we had Dad's S-10 truck loaded down with tools, books, old work clothes, some small pieces of furniture, and my big junk trunk. Mom said if we were lucky Dad would lose it and we wouldn't have to worry about unpacking it. She'd never liked my junk trunk, mostly because I had at least two dozen snakeskins in it that I'd found in the yard over the years. Why a woman who didn't flinch at a dead body feared something as harmless as a snakeskin was beyond me.

The next morning, Dad gave Mom a long kiss good-bye and took off for Armadillo,

Arkansas. Mom and I had to stay behind and pack, which meant that she and Dad wouldn't see each other for two whole weeks. My parents had never spent a night apart. For a long time after Dad was gone, Mom stood at the edge of the yard, staring at the distant spot where his truck had disappeared and where Primrose Lane—the street that had always been the center of my world—narrowed to an end.

We'd never moved before, and I didn't realize how much work was involved. Once we got started, Mom didn't have time to miss Dad. If we weren't eating or sleeping, we were packing something. I wrapped so many pictures and dishes in newspaper that I thought my hands would be ink stained forever. By the end of the two weeks I didn't care if I ever saw another cardboard box.

Mom worried over pointless stuff the whole time. Because we were moving everything in one trip, we could only take what was important. We had to either give away or throw away what was left. That meant the local Goodwill got a lot of our old dishes, books, and clothes, but not until Mom agonized over what to do with each piece of junk.

For example, one day Mom asked me to bag up all the old clothes from the storage closet so we could take them to the Goodwill drop box. I'd filled four extra large trash bags by the time I was ready to clear the top shelf. It had nothing on it but shoes and shoe boxes. One shoe box was red and smaller than the others. I opened it and found a doll-sized white cotton dress with white ribbon rosebuds, a white lace cap, and white knit booties.

"Kevin!" Mom screamed. "What are you doing with that box?" She jerked it away from me. "Don't you dare throw that away."

"What did I do?" I shouted back. "You told me to clean out the closet. I was just looking at it. What's the big deal, anyway? It's only some old doll clothes."

She put the lid back on the box. Her hands trembled. "I guess I'm jumpy about the move."

I didn't like getting yelled at for helping with a move I didn't want to make in the first place. But if Mom didn't care whether I wanted to move or not, why should she care if I thought her yelling was unfair?

Then there was this old ceramic fruit statue Dad's great-aunt Juanita had given her as a wedding gift. Juanita had taken a ceramics class at the assisted living home and painted the statue herself. The problem was Juanita's ninety-year-old eyes were so bad she couldn't have seen an elephant if it sat across from her in a booth at the Dairy Queen. So instead of looking like normal fruit, the statue's orange apples, brown oranges, and bananas the color of cooked spinach looked more like fruit ready for the compost pile.

Mom hated the statue, but she'd kept it because she didn't want to hurt Juanita's feelings—even though Juanita had been dead for eight years.

The statue sat on top of the TV for several days as we packed. Every time Mom walked past it, her jaw tightened and a screeching-tires sound eked out through her clenched teeth.

On the day we packed up the den, I helped Mom disassemble the lamps. I knew something would have to be done about the fruit. Mom would never make the decision if I didn't push her. So I nodded toward the statue. "Why don't you bury that thing in the backyard?"

Mom shook her head. "I couldn't do that." She picked up a lamp shade and covered it with plastic wrap. "Juanita worked so hard on it. I couldn't hurt her feelings."

"How would she ever find out?" I asked. "She died when I was four."

Why she had never thought of that before, I don't know. But now this bit of logic flipped a switch in Mom's brain. Her face glowed from the light of my bright idea. She put the wrapped shade in the box with the others and sealed it with packing tape. "You're right," she said. "I'd forgotten that she died."

I laughed. "That's dumb. You don't forget someone's dead."

"I didn't mean it that way," Mom said. She snatched the statue from the top of the TV. "I guess I don't think about Juanita's death. I love her and think about her as if she were here."

Mom left the room. I heard the front screen door creak open, then slam shut. A few seconds later, there was a sharp crash as the sad fruit statue hit the bottom of the big metal dumpster out front.

Chapter Two

The sun hadn't come up yet when Mom backed the U-Haul out of the driveway and we took off for Armadillo. I didn't know you could burn rubber in a U-Haul. Mom pressed the pedal to the floor and drove through the sleepy neighborhood at least twenty miles over the speed limit. She missed Dad and obviously didn't care if she got a ticket—she just wanted to get to wherever he was, quickly. Since they'd always done everything together, I figured he missed her just as much.

Once Mom merged the U-Haul onto the interstate, any hope I had of the move being just a bad dream was gone. So I decided not to think about it. I wouldn't think about how I'd been forced to leave all my friends behind so my parents could run a rest stop for stiffs. I turned on the radio and gave Mom a brilliant fake smile. She looked surprised at first, then relieved, and gave my hair a tousle with her free hand.

Minutes passed like hours as I watched the asphalt roll under us and the horizon turn pink ahead of us. When the sun finally filtered out the last of the purple dawn, and the sky was as blue as the pool at the Y, we pulled into the Starvin' Marvin off exit 36, halfway to Armadillo. Mom filled up the U-Haul while I bought breakfast to go—two cherry colas, two ham-and-egg biscuits with cheese, and two Hunk-O-Choklit bars.

My biscuit was so dry that when I tried to talk crumbs spewed out of my mouth and flew all over the inside of the cab. Mom found this hilarious, but distracting. Since it took real concentration on Mom's part to eat and drive at the same time, we agreed to eat our biscuits and slurp our cherry colas in silence.

When I was ready for dessert, I tried to guess which end of the Hunk-O-Choklit bar I should start on. Hunk-O-Chocklits were my favorite candy bars: thick as a brick and chunky too, but with pockets of gooey chocolate cream inside. Because the name was molded into the bar, I always ate Hunk-O-Choklit bars from the H down, for good luck. So, like a thousand other times before, I opened the foil wrapper. But this time, instead of finding the "H" like always, I was faced with a "T."

No big deal, I thought. *That's being superstitious—playing a little kid's game such as which way to eat a candy bar.* I took the bar out of its wrapper and turned it around so the H stared up at me, begging to be eaten. Then I rewrapped the foil around the T end and pretended I'd gotten it right the first time.

Determined not to think about this sign of bad luck, I slowly bit into each letter—H, U, N, and K—and listened to my teeth cut through the crunchy bits and felt the gooey part ooze out onto my lips. But when I reached the O, I realized I'd never asked Mom where in Armadillo we were going to live.

"So, Mom," I said, then paused to let my teeth sink into the center of the O. I let the candy melt into a soft puddle on my tongue, so when I spoke again I sounded like I had a bad cold. "Whad's our new houde like? Id it big?"

Mom thought for a minute—another omen I shouldn't have ignored, because it meant she was choosing her words carefully. "Well, we're not actually living in a house."

I chewed the consonant blend CH and swallowed, unaware of the impending doom. "An apartment will be fun. Especially since we won't have to worry about mowing the lawn."

"There's still mowing to be done, Kev. Landscaping, too. We want the funeral home to be neat and attractive. Outside appearances make an impression." Mom was down to the ice in her cola, and the air in her straw made a loud slurpy sound. "But between the three of us, we can keep it up."

Suddenly I felt warm and generous toward my mother. After all, Dad had said I wouldn't have to be around the bodies. And Mom was trying hard to start her new career. "I wouldn't mind doing some yard work for you after school. I could just ride my bike home afterward, if it's not too far." I took a big bite this time, all of O, K, and L.

"That's what makes this so great. It's going to be so convenient living there."

I popped the last IT of the candy bar in my mouth and imagined the possibilities for making new friends in our apartment building beside our new family business.

Mom wadded her candy wrapper and stuffed it in the empty Starvin' Marvin sack. "Yep," she said, in the kind of lilty tone people use when they're pretending you knew all the time about something, except they know you really didn't. "I think living in the funeral home is a great idea."

My breathing stopped. She'd said "in." Living *in* the funeral home!

So much for warm and generous feelings. My parents had lied to me. Not telling the whole story was the same as a lie. And they didn't tell me because they knew I wouldn't like it.

Anger exploded in my mouth like gunpowder. Words shot out so fast I didn't even know for sure what I'd said—but I knew it was bad, because Mom flinched at the impact. She glared at me with one of her Don't-Mess-

With-Me-Kevin-Andrew-Kirk-Or-You're-Gonna-Get-It looks. As she eased onto the Armadillo exit ramp she laid down the law: There was no need to live anywhere else since the funeral home had a nicely furnished second floor with two bathrooms and a kitchen better than the one in our old house, and I'd better not say anything to discourage my father since our family was taking a big step moving and starting a new business and he was nervous and worried enough as it was, so I'd better swallow it up and get over it.

Her words floated around me like the hairs our old orange cat used to shed—small enough on their own to be easily ignored, but incredibly annoying in large numbers. I wanted to swat them out of my face. I wanted to pretend Mom hadn't just told me we were going to live in a house full of corpses. That was the weirdest thing I'd ever heard in my life. How could I eat dinner knowing someone was decomposing just below the kitchen floor? How could I invite friends over—if I could even find friends now? Who'd want to hang out with someone whose houseguests are in rigor mortis?

Mom ended her speech as we passed the Armadillo city limit sign and pulled up to the red brick pillar and lighted placard welcoming us to the Paramount Funeral Home. My father was there with a shovel and a wheelbarrow full of mulch, planting pansies at the base of the sign.

He was having the time of his life. No one seemed to care that this was the end of mine.

Chapter Three

Mom was right about one thing—the apartment on the top floor of the Paramount was nicer than our old home. The den and kitchen combined to make one large room, and the kitchen had all new appliances. A bay window overlooked the back parking area and the wooded lot just beyond, allowing plenty of morning sun into the den.

There were two bedrooms—one facing the front, and the other up two or three steps in what looked more like a large attic space. I got the attic room. It was twice the size of my small room back home, had a bay window facing the back—just like the den's, but smaller—and an angled ceiling. I figured my parents would want that room, since it was the bigger of the two. But Mom said she hated the carpet. It was purple—a rotten, grape-juice purple. I thought it was great but Mom said it looked like the Kool-Aid man had thrown up in there. Ugly carpet seemed a lame reason for Mom to give up the best room, since all she had to do was replace it with a different color. She was obviously trying to ease her guilty conscience.

Each bedroom had its own bathroom. Mine wasn't much bigger than a closet, but it had a shower stall, a sink just the right size for washing your hands, a lighted medicine cabinet with a mirror, and a set of small shelves above the toilet for towels and things. Mom said that since I had my own bathroom, it was my responsibility to clean it. I could leave toothpaste on the sink and dirty towels on the floor without getting yelled at—as long as it was clean by Wednesdays, Mom's inspection day.

We spent the second week landscaping. Dad had started while waiting for us to move in, but the yard was still a mess. "First impressions are important," he said, "and when people see how we care for the outside, they'll think we take care of what's inside, too."

I figured the first impression people would get when they drove by was that we didn't like to mow. By the time we finished all the mulching and planting out front, there was barely any grass left. Still, it did look nice. The boxwoods and holly bushes, pansies and marigolds, lawn edging and cypress mulch looked as good as any of the professional landscaping in town. Mom even created a sitting area in the back outside the guest kitchen. It had a couple of benches, a path of stepping stones set in river gravel, and a small pond that she stocked with three Japanese koi and some water lilies.

Behind the home a grassy patch stretched from the back parking area to the edge of the woods. The spot was popular with the local wildlife. In the early mornings and late afternoons, I could look out our big bay windows and watch the birds, squirrels, raccoons, and deer hunt for goodies in the grass. On our first trip to Wal-Mart, I bought a twenty-five-pound bucket of wild animal feed. I sprinkled some around, and the next morning the lot was crawling with forest critters. Spying on real animals was more fun than watching staged documentaries on TV. Soon I was feeding the animals every night. I even talked Dad into a couple of birdbaths and some feeders to attract more birds to the backyard zoo.

Some of the animals preferred fresh bugs and worms to the dried corn in the feed. Clawed-out holes began to appear in our new landscaping, and Mom's favorite plants were dying as a result. Mom mentioned this one day as she made small talk with the cashier who checked out our groceries at the Piggly-Wiggly.

"Armadillers. They're lookin' for grubs," the clerk said. She scanned the cans of green beans one at a time. "Tough little boogers, 'cept they ain't too good at crossin' the road."

"I haven't seen any in our yard," Mom said.

The clerk groaned as she hoisted the bucket of laundry detergent over the scanner.

"You probably won't see 'em. They don't come out 'till dark. But you'll see the holes where they been diggin'. They got sharp feet."

"How do I keep them out of the flowers?"

The clerk pointed to the far end of the store. "Aisle thirteen. Get yourself some mothballs.

Armadillers hate the smell. Can't say as I blame 'em. Would rather have moths than the mothballs. But don't be surprised if mothballs don't work. Most people, if they can't get shed of 'em, have to get them electric fences to keep 'em out."

When we got home, Mom set out new plants to replace the dead ones. Then she gave me a box of mothballs and told me to scatter them around in the mulch. The smell of the unopened box would have been enough to keep me away. Our armadillos, however, had developed an immunity to mothballs. When I went outside the next morning, our yard looked like the green for the Armadillo Open golf tournament. Mothballs were everywhere but in the mulch, and the armadillos had used Mom's flowerbeds as concession stands.

Once again, Mom put me on mothball duty. This time I had to gather them all and put them in the dumpster. That evening during supper, I watched through the bay window as the guys from Swat Team Termite and Pest Control installed an ultrasonic pest barrier. The Swat Team crawled around in the bushes and across the mulch in their roach colored uniforms. Their names glowed in bright yellow on their backs: Team Member Steve, Team Member Dave, Team Member Jim. We had just started dessert when Team Member Steve walked up the back steps and knocked on the kitchen door.

Mom opened the door. Team Member Steve held out a clipboard and pen. "If you'll sign this, ma'am, we'll be on our way."

Mom signed the bill. Team Member Steve yanked it off the board with a flourish and handed it to her. "Thanks for calling the Swat Team, ma'am. You have a good night."

Mom sat back down to finish her dessert. Dad picked up the bill. He stared at it, his face paler than usual. "Freda, didn't you ask them how much this would cost before you agreed to it?"

Mom leaned over her cherry cheesecake so she wouldn't have to look up at Dad. "We didn't have a choice. We can't have armadillos digging around, tearing up all our work. We've already spent too much money on the landscaping to let them ruin the rest of it."

The air conditioner kicked in with a loud *ha-wumph,* but my parents didn't need any help. There was already plenty of chill in the air. Dad left his half-eaten cheesecake on the table and walked out the back door. I heard each heavy step as he slumped down the stairs. When he reached the bottom, I saw him walk toward the road, hands in his pockets, chin to his chest.

Mom just sat there, leaning over her dessert, her fork stuck in the cake. A tear slid over her cheekbone and hit her plate with a soft splat.

I dumped the rest of my cake in the garbage disposal and went to my room.

Chapter Four

A few days later, Dad and I went to Bigelow's Men's Store in downtown Armadillo. He said if I was going to help them with visitations and funerals, I'd have to dress the part.

Dad picked out five suits for himself—two black, two dark blue, and one gray—plus several white oxford shirts. Then I followed him to the young men's section. I tried on several combinations of coats and slacks before we found the right sizes. He told me to choose two suits that I liked—one black and one dark blue—and he grabbed three white shirts, made just like his, but in my size, off the rack.

We made our way over to the ties. Dad said he preferred paisley prints and stripes, but I could pick out my own. Since my parents had given me no choice but to move—and were now going to make me wear stiff, itchy suits—I decided this would be a good chance to make a statement. So I dug through the bargain bin until I found the five ugliest ties ever made: a dark green one with a painted-on, piranha-looking fish head; one in neon yellow; another in the same throw-up purple as my bedroom carpet; one with pinto beans printed over an orange background; and a black one with a white stripe down the center, like a skunk's back.

Dad never said a word when I dumped the ties on the counter. He did look kind of sick, though, when he heard the total. Still, he pulled out his gold card, handed it to the clerk, and said if you're going to be a funeral director, you've got to wear a nice suit.

On the way home, we stopped at the Cow Palace and ate lunch. Through the window beside our booth, we could see cows out in the field and, up the hill, a big gray barn with a metal roof. I ordered the quarter-pound Cow Pattie with Cheese and a small Herd of Fries; Dad got the Big Steer, through the garden, with the large Herd of Fries.

We ate in silence for a long time. Then after the server gave Dad a refill on his Big Trough Dr Pepper he took a big gulp, as if the drink would clear his throat and his thoughts.

"Kev, you've been a lot of help to us," he said. He set the heavy glass down on the table. "Your mom and I appreciate it."

I nodded, my mouth full of cheddar and Cow Pattie.

"When I was a kid, Dad—I mean your granddad—was in the army. We had to move all the time. I decided I'd never move my kids around like that. I hated moving."

"Well, it's been interesting."

Dad put his elbows on the table, rested his chin in his hands, and looked down at his plate. For a second, I felt sorry for him. Maybe he hadn't wanted to move. He was, after all, more worried about the family finances than Mom. Besides, Mom was the one who wanted to be a funeral director.

"I've been thinking," he said. His eyes were fixed on his last two fries. "I wish we'd let you in on everything from the beginning. I told your mother not to say anything to you about our plans to live in the funeral home."

"Why?" I hadn't expected Dad to be the one to keep a secret from me.

"I didn't want to tell you because I knew you wouldn't like it. That wasn't fair. Even if you didn't like it, at least we should have been honest with you."

"Well, Dad, you're right. I don't like it. It wasn't fair. And I wish you'd been honest." *There,* I thought. *I may have to live where you want to, but now you know I am old enough to express my opinion, whether you like it or not.* I took another bite of my burger.

Dad stirred his drink with his straw. "If your mom and I don't take a chance and make a change in our lives, we'll both be stuck at dead-end jobs. We wanted to work together, and we decided running a funeral home would be our best option, since I already had my degree and some experience."

My jaw dropped, exposing a mouthful of smushed beef. *Dad was an undertaker too?* I thought I knew everything about my parents. Dad motioned at me to close my mouth. I swallowed.

"When did that happen?"

"I met your mom during my last six months of school. I was already apprenticed."

"Why'd you quit? If you spent all that time and money to go to school and be a mortician, why did you go to work at the factory instead?"

Dad gazed out at the cows. One of them, along with her calf, moved close to the window. The calf nuzzled her mother's udder and began to drink.

"I changed jobs a few months after your mom and I married. Before you were born. But that's in the past." Dad sat back and turned his face up to the light fixture made of cowbells that hung over the booth. He exhaled as if he'd been holding his breath for years. "We have you, and we need to plan a future for ourselves now."

Dad's eyes were red, and he rubbed them with the heels of his palms like he does whenever he has a headache. I didn't understand what he meant about changing jobs being in the past, but I felt awkward about asking for an explanation, so I didn't.

"I don't mind helping you or Mom," I said. "I do like my room, and Mom was right about how nice the living area is. But how can I ever have friends over? Who would want to visit me in a funeral home? And I've never even seen anyone dead before. Living in a house with dead people sounds like something out of a creepy old movie."

The longer I talked, the more edgy I felt—and the more droopy and tired Dad looked. I didn't want to spoil his apology, especially since it seemed sincere. So I paused for a moment and calmed down before speaking again. "It's going to be different, that's all. I'm just not sure about it yet."

Dad reached into his pocket, dug out some change for the tip, and placed it on the table beside the ketchup bottle. "Whether we like it or not, death is a part of life." He looked out the window again at the cow. Her calf had finished drinking and was trotting up the hill on spindly legs. "We have to learn to deal with it. Now we'd better get back home. I've got to explain to your mother why I let you buy those wild ties and make her promise not to return them." He slid out of the booth and walked over to the cashier to pay the bill.

"That'll be $11.29," the cashier said. She made eye contact with Dad and smiled. "Say, you're the guy who just bought the Paramount, aren't you? It's the only funeral home in the county, you know. White County only has one, too—in Gleason, the county seat. The Paramount's been here as long as I can remember. The old owners seemed to lose interest in it. I guess the jobs at the new power plant across the river were too tempting."

"The advantage of working with the dearly departed, ma'am," Dad answered with a straight face and a tip of an invisible hat, "is that I don't worry about getting laid off. There's always a job for an undertaker!"

As he and the cashier laughed over his lame joke, I stood by the gum-ball machines at the door and wondered if it was normal for morticians to kid around about their work.

Chapter Five

On July 31 at 3:00 P.M., the Paramount Funeral Home opened for business. The chairperson of the board of directors of the Armadillo Chamber of Commerce, armed with a pair of giant ceremonial scissors, cut the thick blue ribbon that stretched from one front porch column to the other. The ribbon hit the ground, and a small group of business people cheered. The local newspaper photographer took pictures for the *Armadillo Courier.* Mom and Dad exchanged hugs—and sighs of relief that the days of preparation were over.

The next morning Dad backed the hearse out of the garage and left to pick up our first customer: a man named Cletus McCulley, who had passed away at the Shady Grove

Nursing Home and Rehabilitation Center. After Mom and I got the apartment in order, ate a quick breakfast, and cleaned up the dishes, we went downstairs.

Mom's fingers fumbled through the keys until she found the one that opened the front office. It was time to prepare the new desk for the first batch of paperwork, and Mom seemed excited and scared all at the same time. She sent me to the guest kitchen with orders to fill a cut-glass vase with some flowers from the yard and set it on the counter, stock the vending machines with sodas and bottled water, and start the coffeepot.

As I loaded the cans and bottles into the machines, I wondered why a funeral home would need a kitchen in the first place. Chowing down after viewing a dead relative didn't sound appetizing. I could understand the drinks, since people do get thirsty. But why have an extra wide refrigerator, a stove, and a microwave? And enough tables in the room to make it look like a small restaurant?

I got my answer a couple of hours later as I centered the last flower-filled vase on the last table. (Mom said to fix one for the counter, but I got carried away.) Groups of women began marching in, bearing bags and boxes of food for Mr. McCulley's family and friends to eat during the visitation and after the funeral. Soon the countertops were covered with cakes, pies, breads, bags of potato chips, and boxes of cookies and doughnuts. Mom chatted with the women and helped them put the food away.

Dad beeped in on her two-way radio. "Freda, I need your help. Meet me at the service entrance."

She excused herself and headed for the door. "Kevin, please help these women carry in the rest of their things. I'll be back in a minute."

One of the women approached me. She looked to be the same age as Mom, but I'd never seen anyone my mother's age with hair so white. It was lighter than bleached cotton, and hung down the middle of her back and past her waist in a long, bulky braid.

"So your name is Kevin. Well, Kevin, could I get you to help me bring in a few things from my car?" she asked as she got her keys from her purse.

"Sure," I said. I followed her to her car. She had two large flower arrangements crammed in the small backseat. I grabbed the one with the baseball-sized white chrysanthemums. A plastic pick with *Grandfather* in silver letters peeked out from the center of the plants.

She picked up the other arrangement, a spray of pink and yellow roses, and we walked back to the building. "So you're new in town. Are you ready to start school next week?"

"I don't know. I guess so."

"What grade will you be in?"

"Seventh."

"I guess I'll be seeing you, then," she said. We put the flowers on the metal cart in the hall and she held out her hand. "I'm Nancy Goldwyn, the principal at Armadillo Middle. Come by before the first day, and I'll show you around. After my grandfather's funeral, of course." Her eyes were bright and honest blue, and she had the kind of smile that could make you think she never said a bad word about anybody. "It's been very nice to meet you."

"Thanks. You too," I said, and then because I felt like I should, added, "I'm, well, I'm sorry about your grandfather." But it sounded awkward, and the words stumbled over one another.

Mrs. Goldwyn looked past me, but she wasn't focused on anything. I noticed the rims of her eyes were soft pink. "Grandfather lived a good life. He's not sick anymore—probably feels better than he has in years. It's actually a relief to know he's not suffering. And he's with Gran. She died four years ago, and he's missed her terribly."

Despite the sad conversation, she smiled, and we exchanged good-byes again.

After the last group of women left, I found Mom pacing up and down the hall, waving her paper and pencil, her tongue clicking like when we packed for the move.

If she was this whacked out for our first funeral, I wondered, how could she handle several funerals in a week?

"Kev, here's a list of things you need to do. We've been over these before. Eventually we'll get a routine going so we won't need these lists.

Do these ASAP—I've got to get back to the basement." She stuck the paper in my hand and took off for the stairs, ticking like a time bomb.

The list was made up of simple things that I didn't mind doing: put all the flowers in the front of the chapel; prepare the seating; vacuum the front hall. So I pushed the cart with Mrs. Goldwyn's flowers on it through the double doors and down the center aisle between the pews. I placed the flowers on the stands on the left side of the room. I wiped down the backs and ends of the pews with a lemony-smelling dust cloth. The immediate family would sit in the first few rows, so I draped the red velvet covers with *Reserved* embroidered in gold over the arms of those pews. I checked to see that the padded folding chairs in the back of the chapel were lined up straight. Then I vacuumed the entrance hall.

A van from Armadillo Florist and Greenhouse pulled up to the front door. I showed the deliveryman where to put the flowers, and then I went to the guest kitchen for a soda. Mom said I was entitled to free sodas, so I helped myself to a ginger ale. The smell of the food brought in earlier made my stomach growl. I looked at the clock on the wall and discovered it was after six.

Dad walked in, grabbed a diet soda from the machine, and sat down beside me. "I just ordered some pizza," he said. He popped the top on his can. "I don't know about you, but I'm starving. I took a peek in the chapel. It looks good. Have you seen all the flowers in there?"

"I let the guy in to deliver them, but I didn't see them. I came in here to get a drink."

"They're gorgeous. McCulley must have had a lot of friends."

I thought about what Mrs. Goldwyn had said and decided he probably did.

"One more thing. If you'll put McCulley's name and information on the board out front, you can quit for today. I have to go back downstairs and help your Mom finish him up. Then we'll take a breather too."

We'd been so busy I hadn't even thought about what Mom and Dad were doing to Cletus McCulley down in the dungeon.

Suddenly my ginger ale didn't taste so good, and I wasn't so sure I wanted pizza for dinner anymore.

"The family's coming back at eight to plan the service. The visitation starts tomorrow afternoon at three, so I imagine the funeral will be the day after. When you fix the message board, just put the name and time for the first visitation."

Mom beeped, interrupting our break. Dad drank the last of his soda and got up to leave. "Don't forget the pizza," he said. He pulled out his wallet, thumbed through what little cash he had, decided which bills he could give up, and tossed them onto the table. Then as an afterthought, he pitched one more on the pile. "Give the driver a tip."

Mom beeped again, impatient for Dad to get back to the basement. The pizza guy buzzed in at the front entrance. "Don't eat all the hot peppers!" I heard Dad yell as he descended the stairs.

I walked down the hall to the front double doors. I could smell the crust even before I turned the doorknob. "One 'Feed Four for

$14.99 Special' with extra peppers," said the pizza guy like he'd been saying it all day. "That'll be $15.89."

I counted out nineteen bucks and handed it over. "That's stupid to sell pizza for four for $14.99 and then charge $15.89."

"Tax," the pizza boy said, and yawned. "Thanks for the tip."

I took the pizza and started up the stairs to my room. The bottom of the box was hot and moist, and I could almost taste the Italian sausage. I wondered why Dad ordered enough pizza for four people when there were only three of us in the house who could eat it.

Chapter Six

After supper I got the key from the desk and opened the glass door covering the message board. The board was made of grooved black plastic, and there was a brand-new box of white plastic letters with points on the back that stuck into the grooves. I sorted through them and took out enough letters to spell:

CLETUS DARNELL MCCULLEY
VISITATION WED. 3–8 PM

By then the sky had turned peachy. I filled a jug with water, grabbed the bucket of wild animal feed, and headed for the back lot. The frogs and crickets muffled the sounds of the few cars that passed on the highway out front. I dumped the old water out of the birdbaths, poured fresh water from the jug, and then started sprinkling feed on the ground.

A soft voice spoke up behind me. "Look, Kevin!" It was Mrs. Goldwyn. She pointed to the trees.

A doe stood about twenty feet from us, just beyond the pines at the edge of the woods. I moved forward to get a closer look, but I stepped on a twig, snapping it in two. The noise startled the doe and she leapt away, blending into the foliage.

"This must be a good spot to see animals," Mrs. Goldwyn said. "Especially since you offer free food and drinks."

"We have lots of squirrels and raccoons. Sometimes a deer or two." I threw a handful of feed toward the trees. "And there's always birds. Early morning is the best time to see any of the animals."

"There must be armadillos around here."

"I've only seen dead ones on the side of the road," I said. "The live ones were coming out at night and digging up Mom's plants. She had to call the pest control guys 'cause the armadillos were ruining our landscaping."

Mrs. Goldwyn reached into my bucket, grabbed a handful of feed, and pitched it underhanded into the air. The seeds scattered and fell a short distance away.

"We're making the arrangements for Grandfather's funeral. My husband is meeting with your parents right now. I saw you out here and thought I'd see what you were doing. It was a good excuse to get some fresh air." She took a deep breath and glanced over her shoulder, as if she suddenly remembered she'd left something inside. The abrupt silence was awkward, so I pretended to pick bad seeds out of the feed bucket.

I had almost a fistful of seeds by the time she spoke up again. "Your family has made this place look nice. The old owners didn't care about it like your parents do."

I pitched the imperfect seeds toward the woods. "Dad says he likes working with Mom. Says it's better than his old factory job."

"Your mom told me she couldn't have done any of this without your help."

I kicked at a dirt clod with my toe and mumbled a thank-you. I figured she didn't have to know how I really felt about it.

"Would you mind coming in with me for a minute? There's someone I'd like you to meet."

Mrs. Goldwyn waited for me while I put the jug and the feed away. We walked through Mom's garden and entered the building through the guest kitchen. Then I followed her down the entrance hall and through the chapel doors.

The room was thick with flowers. The heat from the bright lights in front of the chapel intensified their colors, and the air was so fragrant that if you closed your eyes you'd think you were outside. Halfway down the aisle, I realized Mrs. Goldwyn and I were the only two living people in the room.

"It's OK, Kevin," she said. "I just want you to meet my grandfather."

She was talking about this dead body like it was alive! The chapel doors tugged at me like giant magnets. The urge to back up made my legs quiver.

"Please, Kevin," she pleaded. "Please come with me."

Then she smiled that smile again, the same one she gave me the first time we talked. Now

I felt guilty—and stupid—for wanting to run. So I decided I wouldn't think about the fact that I was about to see a dead body. I'd pretend it was something else, like a mannequin.

I let her lead me forward again, but I kept my eyes glued to the large portrait beside the casket. It was of an elderly couple, seated close together. Gold letters at the bottom of the frame spelled out *50th Anniversary.* The woman was round and red-cheeked. The man had his arm around her shoulders. He was built like a concrete block, with skin that had spent a lifetime in the sun. His snow-white crew cut fit his head like a cap; his smile was a perfect match to Mrs. Goldwyn's. And his eyes—

Inside his ordinary face, the man's eyes sparkled with the color of a cloudless Easter Sunday when the sun is hot, the air is cool, and the sky opens up into forever. They looked through me and traced up and down the edges of my spine like two pieces of cold, blue steel.

Cletus McCulley knew me.

Mrs. Goldwyn gave me a gentle nudge. We'd reached the front of the chapel. She rested her hand on the edge of the casket. "Kevin, this is my grandfather."

Cletus McCulley was dressed in a white suit, every white hair in his army-regulation crew cut stiffly in place, his arms stretched out at his sides. His eyelids were frozen shut and his lips stretched tight, like he was holding his breath. The lights above the casket gave his skin a slight orange undertone.

I couldn't pretend he was a mannequin, because he didn't look like one. But he didn't look like a living person. He looked like his picture, except he didn't look warm. But he wasn't cold, purple, or decayed, the way corpses looked in movies.

Mrs. Goldwyn's voice floated like a milkweed puff. "No one can tell you what death is like, so it's easy to be afraid of it."

I kept waiting for his big, broad chest to expand with breath. It looked as if it would move any second. But it didn't.

"See those medals?" She pointed to an oak box on a small stand beside the casket. "Grandfather served in World War II. He rarely talked about the war, but he told me once that one of his buddies died after being hit by sniper fire in a French village, after the Normandy invasion. His friend died in his arms, and Grandfather said that was a sacred moment."

Sacred. I thought people only used that word when talking about the Bible. Not that I knew much about the Bible, but somehow, even though I'd never heard anyone use the word *sacred* when talking about death, it seemed right.

Mrs. Goldwyn stroked the satin lining of the casket. "When Gran died he held her too, and had those same feelings. I believe when Grandfather's spirit left his tired, sick body behind, that was his sacred moment."

Cletus's chest still didn't move, but an easy warmth swelled in mine. I'd always thought if you were dead, you were all dead. Was there something inside people that didn't die when their bodies did? My eyes went back to the portrait. "Where do you think he is now?"

"He'll stay as close to us as he can, in spirit." A tear slipped from her left eye as she reached into the casket to smooth an imaginary wrinkle on her grandfather's shirt. "But now he's back with Gran and the friends who died before him. That's what Grandfather and Gran taught me, from the time I was a little girl. And I believe it." Mrs. Goldwyn put her arm around me and gave me a squeeze. "Today, I believe it more than ever."

I looked down at Cletus McCulley's body again. The fear and disgust I'd expected to feel wasn't there at all. It was a quiet calm instead, like the time our old orange cat gave birth in the tool shed. It was as if the earth stopped turning for a few minutes, just long enough for someone unseen to open a window as each squirming, wet kitten appeared. I watched the mother as she licked them clean, and wondered how there could be five wiggly fur balls when a few moments earlier there'd been none. They had to come from somewhere. But where, I didn't know.

Maybe Cletus, or what was inside his body that made him Cletus—his spirit?—had moved to a place I couldn't see, a place like where the kittens came from. Maybe he was standing at an open window with his wife right now. Maybe he was listening to our conversation and bragging to his friends about how his granddaughter's smile was just like his.

Sorry I didn't get to talk to you, Kevin, but I had to go. Glenda Sue was getting impatient!

I shook my head hard and rubbed my hand over my temples. The lights were too hot, and it was getting too late. And who was Glenda Sue?

That night, the first night we had a dead body downstairs, I dreamed I was inside a white mansion, wandering through white halls filled with flowers and crawling with newly weaned kittens. The kittens were all different colors and mewed to be held, licking at my bare feet and ankles with their small sandpaper tongues.

Chapter Seven

The next evening I took my post at the front entrance. Dressed in my new dark blue suit and fish-head tie, my black hair combed straight (except for that annoying cowlick to the left of my forehead), I was ready to open the door for visitors. Mom frowned when she saw the tie, but she didn't say anything.

By the time visiting hours started, our parking lot was fuller than Wal-Mart's on a Saturday night. About every half hour, Mom gave me a short break, so I didn't get too tired. I didn't get bored, either; it was interesting to watch people as they came in and out of the home.

I got to meet Mrs. Goldwyn's husband. He was at least seven feet tall and an ex-basketball player—for the Razorbacks while in college, then for the Lakers until he got tired of L. A. and traveling so many months out of the year. He said Mrs. Goldwyn's smile dragged him back home to Arkansas.

Mrs. Goldwyn also introduced me to President Carter, who would conduct the funeral the next day. Like Dad, he was almost bald. But President Carter's remaining hair was carrot-colored, and he stood at least a foot taller. When he shook my hand, his grip was sure and strong.

"It's nice to meet you, Kevin. Your parents have told me a lot about you."

Great, I thought. *I'll bet they told Cletus McCulley all about me too, while they were embalming him.* So I just smiled and said thanks.

"You may be in some classes with my daughter this year," he said. He looked around the room. "She's here somewh—"

A slender finger tapped his shoulder. "Oh, here she is," he said, and pulled her around to face me. "Dani, this is Kevin Kirk."

Dani blushed. She held out her hand and ducked her head slightly. She eyed me through the rims of her antique-gold eyeglasses. Her bangs brushed across the top of the frames. "Hi, Kevin."

"Hi," I answered. Her hand felt warm and delicate, like I was holding a baby bird. I hoped I didn't squeeze too hard.

"You and I may see a lot more of each other, Kevin," President Carter said. "I visit the funeral home often. Sometimes I conduct services for families who aren't members of our church."

I was still shaking Dani's hand. I let go.

"If you'll excuse us," President Carter said, "I have to speak to Sister Goldwyn about the music for tomorrow. We'll talk to you again soon." Dani held the sleeve of her father's suit coat as they walked away, but she looked back at me over her shoulder and flashed a shy smile. I saw a glimmer between her lips and realized she wore braces.

President was a strange title for a preacher. I asked Mom about it, and she said President Carter was a Mormon branch president. Mormon—or Latter-day Saint—branch presidents were like preachers except they weren't paid to oversee their congregations, so they had regular jobs like most people. I also thought Mormons didn't drink coffee. I'd seen several people in the guest kitchen helping themselves. Mom said Mrs. Goldwyn had asked her to have coffee on hand because many of her grandfather's friends weren't Mormons.

It was strange, too, that most everyone at the visitation acted happy. Some looked bluer than others, but no one cried or moaned or wailed. There was lots of hugging and sympathetic cheek-kissing between family, friends, and neighbors. Some people called each other brother and sister.

As the night wore on, a group of old men gathered in the back of the chapel. At one point there must have been fifteen of them. They were all enthusiastic fishermen, and Cletus had been a part of their group. Someone started in on all the good times he'd had fishing with Cletus, and before long all the old men in the back were howling. That didn't set well with the somber old women in the front, and a couple of puckery-faced ones turned around to shush them.

However, the old men were on a roll and weren't about to let Cletus's fish tales rest in peace. I was glad, because I was having a good time eavesdropping. One of the men was a really good storyteller, and before I knew it he had me hooked—especially as he told the one about the time Cletus thought he'd caught a water moccasin on his line. It was really just a harmless water snake, but it scared Cletus so bad that he jumped backward and stumbled over his seat. The boat flipped, and Cletus, his tackle box, and brand new Zebco rod fell into the lake. Cletus, thinking the snake was mad and in swift pursuit behind him, swam to shore as fast as a seventy-year-old man with a stomach the size of a watermelon could swim. When he reached the muddy bank, it was so slick he had to crawl on his knees to get out of the lake. Thinking he could frighten the snake away, he hollered, "Oooh! Oooh! Oooh!" and beat his chest with his muddy hands, like some kind of white-haired Ozark gorilla.

The picture of a fat old man sitting in the mud and beating his chest like a gorilla was just too funny. The storyteller caught my snicker and waved his arm at me. "C'mere, boy," he said, and motioned me into the chapel. Afraid I was in trouble, I left my post at the door and approached the group, sheepish and redfaced.

The storyteller pulled me close to his chair and gave me a good-natured slap on the back. "Now this is a boy who knows a good fish tale when he hears it. Why lookie here," he said, giving my tie a yank, "he even wears a fish around his neck!" The other old men in the group nodded their approval. They were all wearing Old Spice, and the smell was overpowering. "What's your name, son?"

Relieved to know I wasn't going to get yelled at, I spoke up. "Kevin. Kevin Kirk."

"You're the boy of the man that runs this place, aren't you? Well, you're all doing a fine job. Here, let me give you something." He reached into his pocket and pulled out a purple plastic worm. It was fat and had silver and red sparkles embedded in it. "Cletus always carried bait on him. We called him the Armadillo Angler, 'cause he'd drop whatever he was doin' if he thought the fish were bitin'.

You keep this in your pocket too. You never know when you'll get a chance to cast your line in Armadillo. And you can tell everybody Herb Conrad shared his bait with you."

"Thanks, Mr. Conrad," I said, turning the worm around in my hand, making the light glint off the sparkles. I'd never owned a fishing worm before. It was slightly sticky and smelled funny, but in a way it was interesting to look at. Maybe that's why they were so tempting to the fish.

The other men in the group introduced themselves, and each shook my hand. I wanted to hear more stories, but Mom whisked me away to the kitchen to restock the soda machine.

After the funeral the next morning, the rest of the day was quiet. Mom felt we needed to evaluate our progress, so that night we all sat around the kitchen table to discuss business: Mom in her fuzzy frog house shoes and orange terrycloth robe, Dad in his old gray sweatpants with the hole in the seat and his *See Rock City* T-shirt, and me in the camouflage pants and Army shirt Granddad had given me for Christmas last year.

Mom licked the last bits of dessert off her spoon and rapped it on the table. "The initial meeting of the board of directors of the Paramount Funeral Home will now come to order. What is the first item of business?"

I wanted to make a motion to change the name from Paramount to the Buzzard Bait Motel. But Mom had not only pulled off her first funeral without a hitch, she'd actually made a good tasting chocolate pie for dinner. I didn't have the heart to be mean. Still, would it hurt to look out for the employee's best interest? "How about a raise for your son? Or better yet, when do I get my first paycheck?"

Dad opened up the ledger. When I saw the list of bills they had to pay, I was ashamed for even asking about money. The Swat Team visit—and Dad's stunned expression from that night—flashed through my mind. The muscles in my chest tightened, and I felt pangs of remorse.

Dad pulled a fifty out of his wallet and laid it on top of the ledger. "We've been holding this back for you. Without your help, we couldn't have done all this. Still, money is going to be tight for a while. Would you feel OK about a savings account in your name, where we can deposit your money and you can withdraw a little on occasions when you really need it?"

"Sounds good to me." I tried to make it sound positive, but inside I felt terrible. I pocketed the fifty and promised myself I would make it last as long as I could.

"I've been thinking," Mom spoke up. "What if we give Kev a radio, too? We're always chasing him down. And what if we give him a master list of jobs? That way we won't have to come up with a new list every time."

"Motion seconded," said Dad. "All in favor—"

"Aye!" Mom and I shouted together.

Dad's tone then turned serious. "Now once school starts, your first priority is homework. Anything you do here comes second."

"OK, Dad."

"We do need you, but not at the expense of your grades. You're too good of a student to slack off," Mom said.

I groaned. "I know, Mom."

"One more thing, before I forget." Mom spoke as if she were in a hurry. "Arlice, President Carter offered to conduct funeral services for people who need a minister but don't attend any church. I thought that was a good idea, so I told him we'd call on him."

Dad gave Mom a funny look. "Why'd you do that for?"

"Well, he offered, and you know he doesn't accept money for preaching funerals." Mom was trying to pass the conversation off as if it were nothing. "I thought it was a nice gesture."

Dad looked uncomfortable. Why would it bother him for President Carter to offer help? "I think it's nice too, Dad," I spoke up. Now Mom looked at *me* funny, but I guess she was surprised that I agreed with something she said. She didn't have to know I was hoping for another chance to talk to President Carter's daughter.

"Well, whatever," Dad said. "As far as I'm concerned, this meeting is now adjourned because. . ." His voice trailed off as he looked at his watch, "it's time for the *Twilight Zone!*"

Mom rolled her eyes and hugged me goodnight. Dad grabbed a Dr Pepper and a bag of cheese popcorn and headed for the couch.

"G'night, Dad," I called to the couch.

"G'night, son," Dad called back, his voice muffled by cheese popcorn and the dee-dee-dee-dee of the *Twilight Zone* theme.

I went to my room. I used the bathroom and didn't flush, then brushed my teeth and left the cap off the toothpaste. When I set the tube down, a blob of turquoise gel oozed onto the white porcelain sink. I washed my face, and let my towel drop to the floor. Then I went to bed, and until I got sleepy, I watched through the window as the deer and raccoons fed out in the back lot.

Maybe life in the Buzzard Bait Motel wasn't going to be so bad after all.

But then, I thought as I rolled over and closed my eyes, *school hasn't started yet.*

Chapter Eight

The funeral home was quiet for a few days after Cletus McCulley was buried, which was nice because we all needed a rest. On Saturday, Dad took Mom out to the weekend catfish buffet at the Cow Palace. On Monday, Dad and I checked out the middle school. The building was covered in flaky old bricks that looked like they would crumble if you spit on them. Mrs. Goldwyn had a meeting out of town, so I didn't get a tour, but Dad paid my locker fees and book fees and I got signed up for classes.

Afterward, we went shopping for school clothes and supplies. I hated buying school clothes, and this year was no exception. I picked out three pairs of plain khakis, three pairs of plain jeans, and four plain shirts. I had no interest in being a walking advertisement, so I purposefully avoided clothes with labels, logos, or tags. I just wanted to look clean.

But when buying school supplies, I couldn't resist any nifty gadget lurking in the Home and Office Equipment aisle. Buying supplies was always my favorite thing about starting a new school year.

I loved going shopping in August, when the stores smelled like new pencils and crayons and the stacks of loose-leaf paper stood taller than Mrs. Goldwyn's husband. I hated homework, but I loved organizing it, and was always able to talk my parents into buying all the binders, notebooks, folders, labels, and mechanical pencils I wanted.

On the way home, we stopped at a small bookstore just on the edge of downtown Armadillo. The public rest rooms at the Paramount were in desperate need of remodeling. While Dad searched for books about do-it-yourself tile replacement, I wandered around the Outdoor Sports section. They had hundreds of books on hunting and fishing. The thought of shooting deer for sport never appealed to me, but after hearing Cletus McCulley's friends talk, I thought fishing might be fun. I bought a book from the bargain bin, *A Beginner's Guide to Fishing in Arkansas,* complete with full-color photographs of native species. The fish on the cover had a mouth big enough to stick your fist into and flat glassy eyes. The caption underneath told me it was *Micropterus salmoides,* otherwise known as a largemouth bass.

On Tuesday, Dad and I went to the barbershop. Now this was one of Dad's quirky habits that made no sense at all. Why get a haircut every other week when the only hair that grows on your head is around the perimeter? I'd seen more fuzz on a marble than on Dad's scalp. For years, I'd watched as barbers would spend thirty minutes or more on Dad's head, snip-snip-snipping away at nothing, yet still charge him for a full-price haircut in the end.

I sat in the chair first and got my usual cut—short and tapered on the sides and back, the thickness cut off the top and combed down to my forehead. I tried a buzz cut once, thinking I'd look like a marine, but since I wasn't old enough to shave yet, I just looked like a stupid kid who'd cut off all his hair. And bowl cuts left my hair too long on the sides. But a fade seemed to work best on my straight black hair, making my cowlick less noticeable, at least until the front grew out.

While the barber worked on me, Dad refereed a debate between two old men about which team was going to win the National League pennant. The barber had just started trimming above my ears when the bell above the door jingled.

"Mr. Kirk," Herb Conrad shouted, "how in the world are you, buddy?"

"Good to see you, Mr. Conrad," Dad shouted back. In the mirror I could see Dad get up from his chair and shake Mr. Conrad's hand. "The boy and I are getting a haircut today. I can't stand a shaggy head," he said, rubbing his bald top and laughing.

"Know what you mean, Kirk. Just makes you feel unclean when your hair gets a little unruly. And how's that son? You think we could make a fisherman out of him?"

Dad pointed at my chair. "Why don't you ask him?"

Mr. Conrad leaned into my face and winked. "You think I could drag you out onto the lake sometime?"

"Sure, Mr. Conrad." I didn't want to sound eager, but it was hard to hold back my enthusiasm.

"Are you still carrying the bait I gave you?"

"Yup." I reached in my pocket and pulled out the worm. "I also bought a book so I could learn the different kinds of fish in Arkansas," I added, hoping he would see I was serious about fishing.

Mr. Conrad laughed. "Boy, you don't learn to fish out of a book." I was embarrassed then, and worried that he thought I was just another dumb kid. But he soon put me at ease. "A book is helpful, Kevin, but you learn by doing. You can read the books all you want, but the way you really learn is by reading the water, the weather, the time of day, and the surroundings. And even then, you might stay out all day and still not catch nothin'. But most of the time, that's the fun in fishing. You don't have to catch a fish to have a good time. 'Cause most of the time, the fun's in just being there."

Soon it was Dad's turn, and we changed seats. The barber tied the drape around Dad's neck and pretended to trim his scalp. I thumbed through a stack of old magazines and pulled out a three-year-old copy of the *National Tattler Weekly*. On the front was the bold headline, "MYSTERIOUS TWO-HEADED GOAT FOUND GRAZING AT GRACELAND," with the caption, "Scientists puzzled by amazing goat marked with Elvis's profile. Full-color pull-out section inside!" And there was the goat, with an inky blob on his butt. Both heads chewed on mouthfuls of straw and smiled at the camera. Someone had removed the full-color center section, so I'd never know for sure if that goat bore the Sign of the King or not.

I peeked over the paper and watched the barber trim the back of Dad's neck. The chair was turned sideways, giving me a good view of Dad's profile. I'd always been told we looked alike. We had the same pale, easily sunburned skin. We both had dark brown eyes, almost black, and thick black eyebrows, like two fat wooly worms, identically arched. Our ears had the same shape and the same fleshy lobes.

Our faces were similar, but at eleven I was already as tall as Dad, and Mom said that when I reached sixteen I'd be even taller. Dad was stocky and muscular like a football player. I was thinner and built like a runner, more like Mom's family.

Those weren't the only differences between Dad and me. Dad was a talker. Yak, yak, yak. He could talk to anyone about anything at just about anytime. Even now, Dad, the barber, and Herb Conrad were having a great time insulting the career politicians in Little Rock who were wasting their constituents' hard-earned money. Mom was a talker too. Grandma Kirk said once that the reason I didn't talk much was because between Mom and Dad, I didn't get much of a chance to say anything.

Grandma Kirk was partly right. Sure, Mom and Dad talked a lot. But that wasn't the whole reason I was quiet. I liked to listen and observe. I thought about things more than I talked about them—except when I got mad. Like the day of the move, when Mom told me we'd be living in the home, I lost my temper, and before stopping to think, I said things I shouldn't have. So while I took pride in being a thoughtful person, I wasn't so proud of being the kind of person who loses his temper so easily.

Dad liked being around people. Mom did too. So I guess the funeral home business was perfect for them. I liked being with friends at school and having them come over occasionally, but I didn't need a lot of company. I enjoyed having time to myself, and felt grumpy if I didn't get it. I decided then that Dad's bi-weekly haircuts were more for his mental health than his personal hygiene. He needed interaction as much as I needed privacy.

But not needing a lot of company wasn't the same as never having company, which was one of many thoughts that rolled around in my mind that night as I tried to go to sleep. I reached over to the nightstand and picked up the fishing worm that Herb Conrad had given me at Cletus McCulley's visitation. I looked at it and wondered why a fish would be so dumb as to think a purple plastic worm would be real food, especially a purple plastic worm with a big silver hook stuck through it. Maybe the glitter imbedded in the plastic made it look tasty. It didn't look tasty to me. But then again, I wasn't a fish.

I remembered the picture on the cover of my new fishing book. *Micropterus salmoides* had a mouth cavity that looked ten times bigger than its brain cavity. No wonder it couldn't tell the difference between a plastic worm and a real one.

I wondered what it would be like to catch a fish and reel it in. Maybe Herb Conrad wouldn't forget me, and would make a real offer to take me fishing sometime.

I imagined Cletus McCulley sitting in a boat out in the middle of a lake, casting a line. He let it arc gracefully across the bright spring sky until the weight of the hook and bait made it sink, then disappear, underneath the water's surface.

I imagined the quiet, glassy ripples rolling from one side of the lake to the other. I smelled the blue-green water, scented by the slimy carpet of algae that separated it from the shore. I warmed my skin in the rays of the mid-May sun.

And I was in the boat, sitting beside Cletus. He offered me a can of soda. I popped the top and the fizz sprayed my face, making me flinch. Cletus laughed. I stuck my tongue out to get the drops between my chin and bottom lip. I wiped the rest of it off with the back of my hand. The spray was sticky and cold, but delicious on what was becoming a hot day.

Cletus then fingered through a pile of rods, picked out a sleek, black, graphite beauty, and passed it to me. When I had the reel end in a firm grip, he let go of the pole and scratched his chin. His lips didn't move, but I heard his voice. *Hmm . . . now what should we bait Kevin's pole with?* He groaned as he leaned over his round, basketball-sized belly to reach the tackle box. He rummaged around in the compartments until he found the perfect artificial bait. *This spinner looks good. Perfect for catching largemouth bass.*

"You mean *Micropterus salmoides,"* I spoke up. "That's the scientific name."

I heard Cletus chuckle in his mind, and I watched his fat fingers thread the line through the loops on the spinner. "It's too bad we didn't get to go fishing while you were alive," I said.

Who says I'm not living? Cletus thought. *I'm sitting here beside you, aren't I?*

"I saw you at the funeral home," I said. "Your granddaughter made me look at your body in the casket. And when was the last time you ever heard of a dead man fishing?"

Cletus finished tying the spinner, and he turned his head toward me with a grandfather-knows-best kind of smile. His blue eyes splashed a wave of cold up my arms and across my face. His mouth opened and the words came out as clean and as sharp as a brand-new filet knife: "There's more to life than what you see."

My body jerked upright. Had I dreamed? Had I dozed off? I felt like I'd been dipped in a vat of ink. My eyes couldn't adjust from the bright dream to the black night. I rubbed my hands over my face and looked at the clock. It was three in the morning. I let my head drop back on the pillow and had barely closed my eyes again when the 5:50 alarm sounded.

I got up, dressed, washed my face, and went out to the back lot. I took a folding stool, a new composition notebook, a mechanical pencil, and a resolve to forget the dream I'd had about Cletus McCulley. It was a dream, after all. Only a dream.

After reading the last issue of *National Geographic*, I'd decided to keep a log of what I saw in the back lot each day and the time I saw it—just like the real biologists. If Armadillo Middle had a school science fair, this would give me a head start on a project. I reached the edge of the parking lot, set up the chair, and settled in. I recorded the date, time, and weather conditions and turned my eyes to the trees and the thick undergrowth.

August 9, 6:14 A.M.

WEATHER: cloudy, slight wind, drizzle

WHAT I SAW:

- Two cardinals
- One squirrel, light gray with short tail (maybe cut or torn off)
- One doe, ran from side of house back into woods
- One green snake (don't tell Mom, she'll freak)
- Several robins

At 7:14 I closed my notebook and folded my stool. I carried them up the stairs to the second floor deck and through the back door. Dad was at the stove, cooking breakfast. "For you," he said, "to help you get started on the first day of school."

The aroma of bacon frying in the hot iron skillet was real. The sweet scent of maple syrup mingled with butter was real too. This wasn't a dream. Dad was making my breakfast, and the breakfast was real right there, sizzling on the stove. I took the plate he offered me plus the half-empty bottle of pancake syrup and sat down at the table.

The problem was, fishing with Cletus McCulley last night was every bit as real as the first bite of bacon I'd just put in my mouth.

Chapter Nine

Armadillo Middle wasn't bad at first. I got in all the right classes without having a screwed-up schedule, and all my teachers seemed OK. Even Mrs. Goldwyn stopped me in the hall the first day, asked how my parents were doing, and how I liked the school.

I'm not the kind of person who makes friends easily. I'm quiet and don't like to hang out in large groups. So the guys, though friendly, didn't have much in common with me, and most of them had little to say other than "hello."

Dani Carter, however, was in all my classes except PE. After a couple of weeks, we found ourselves sharing notes, pairing up for first-quarter projects, and forming an unspoken understanding that whoever entered the classroom or cafeteria first would save a seat for the other.

At first I told myself that even though Dani was a girl, she was better than no friend at all. She wasn't interested in most of the things my old friends and I used to talk about at school, but I soon realized I liked it that way. Before the first half of the grading period was up, I didn't care if I had guy friends or not. Being with Dani, even if we did nothing else but sit together in class, was more fun than pretending I enjoyed discussing pro-wrestling or the latest music CD. Dani liked a lot of the same subjects I did: biology, pre-algebra, and history. But she was a better reader than me, and sometimes it was hard to get her attention if she was into her latest book.

My new-school success didn't last long. When Chuck Stiller showed up for his first day back, I knew he would give me trouble the rest of the year.

Chuck Stiller was smart (smart-mouthed, that is), short (shorter than me, anyway), and he walked with a swagger like Barney Fife in the old *Andy Griffith Show* reruns. Some days he wore shoes, but most of the time he wore boots. No matter which, they were always caked with dried mud. He didn't care that everyone thought of him as the Student Most Likely to Spend Life in Prison. And when Stiller picked a victim, most of the other kids (whether they liked Stiller or not) offered support because they feared being next on his list.

One day in mid-September, I'd taken my seat in first hour when Stiller came in. He'd been sick—or in juvenile detention, I wasn't sure—and ended up coming back to school a lot later than everyone else. He'd intended to find me on his first day back, because as soon as he entered U.S. History, he approached me with a clipping he'd cut from the morning's *Armadillo Courier.* It was an ad for the funeral home, with a picture of my family at the ribbon cutting ceremony.

Stiller waved the clipping under my nose. "So, your mommy's a mortician, huh?"

A dozen kids circled my desk. I started to sweat a little but figured if I played it cool he'd get tired of messing with me and move on. "Yeah, my mom's a mortician, and my dad is too. They just opened the business this summer."

"Ain't that special," he jeered, thrusting the clipping in my face. "That's an awful nice suit you're wearing there. Looks like you want to grow up to be just like Daddy."

The posse surrounding my desk laughed. I tried to ignore my embarrassment. "No, I just help my parents when they need it."

"Is it true, Kevie, you live inside the funeral home?"

"Yes." He wanted to go somewhere with this, and my fists wanted to go somewhere too—right between his eyes.

Stiller exhaled a mock sigh. "You gotta make friends where you can. Since you don't have any friends at school 'cept that Mormon girl," he waved his arm at Dani, "I guess dead friends are better than none at all." By this time the entire class was laughing, except for Dani. She was pretending to read, her head ducked behind *The Story of America: Our History to 1865.*

At lunch, Dani told me to ignore Stiller. Maybe he'd get tired of teasing me after a while, she said. But as I waited for Mom to pick me up that afternoon, Stiller and a new gang stood next to me in line and asked if there was enough room in the hearse for all of them to get a ride home. When Mom pulled up in the S-10, I told her that if she ever picked me up from school in the hearse, I'd leave Armadillo and never come back.

The next day Stiller burst into first hour again. He grabbed my lunch sack and started parading it around the room. "Well, Kevie, what's for lunch today?"

I jumped out of my seat and snatched it back. "Nothing that concerns you."

"What does your mommy do with all those body parts, Kevie?" Stiller snickered, and the class began to roar. "What does she do with all the intestines and stomachs and eyeballs and livers?" He held his nose up in the air and began to sniff. "Could that smell be your lunch, Kevie? Did Mommy fix you a fried brain sandwich?" He grabbed the sack again and ran to the window. He put his free hand up to his throat and began making gagging sounds. "This stinks SOOOO bad, it's makin' me hurl. We've got to get it out of here!"

Stiller stuck his arm out the window, and I heard the sack pop as it hit the concrete two stories below. Our teacher, Mr. Hampton, walked in then and sent Stiller straight to the assistant principal, who gave him two weeks' detention for throwing stuff out the window.

Detention quieted Stiller down for a little while, since getting caught at something else would make his punishment worse. But it did nothing to help me. A few days later I didn't have any trouble finding my locker. It was the one with KANNIBAL KEVIN scrawled on the door in black permanent ink. Clearly, Stiller's seventh-grade project was to destroy my reputation.

At lunch, after our unsuccessful attempt to clean Stiller's artwork off my locker, Dani gave me a pep talk as we sat in a booth in the back of the cafeteria.

"I don't care what Chuck does. I'm your friend. So what if your parents *are* morticians?" Her brown eyes were solemn behind her wire-rimmed glasses. "Somebody has to be. He's just looking for someone to pick on, and you're an easy target because you're new."

I studied Dani's straight brown hair and the bright yellow hair band she'd pulled it back with. It felt odd to sit with a girl, but I liked it. And I liked Dani. Everything about her, from her braces to her white leather sneakers, oozed sincerity. So even if her friendship was the result of being her latest charity project, some support was better than none at all.

The days dragged on, and so did Stiller's relentless teasing. I managed to get through the first quarter with all A's, and Dani and I made the honor roll. So did Stiller. When I searched for my name on the honor roll banner by the front doors, I found someone had marked out my first name and written over it in big black letters, KANNIBAL.

Chapter Ten

I'd never hated anyone before, but I was beginning to hate Chuck Stiller.

I'd never hated school, either. But by Halloween, every day at Armadillo Middle was a living nightmare. My locker was the dump for Stiller's leftover lunch garbage—banana peels, plastic utensils, sandwich scraps, anything he could shove through the vents. After ruining two new pairs of jeans by sitting on gum wads Stiller had planted, I had to check every seat in every class before sitting down. And it seemed like no matter which hall I was in, Stiller was there too, sneering at me and throwing paper wads—or worse.

November proved to be more of the same. A few days before Thanksgiving break, as I waited for Mom to pick me up after school,

Stiller strutted over with his usual crew of spineless onlookers.

"Know something, Kevie?" Stiller stretched his neck so his mouth could reach my ear. "I don't think you like me."

I ignored him.

"I'm talkin' to you, Kevie. Look at me when I'm talkin' to you."

I refused to give him the satisfaction.

"Just a minute," Stiller said. He turned to his audience. "I think Kevie is scared of me! Is that true, Kevie?" He stretched up to my ear again and spoke in baby tongues. "Wittle Kevie-Wevie is afwaid of Chucky-Wuckie? Poor baby." His friends roared. He reached up to pat me on the head and I smacked his arm away.

Breaking my resolve, I whirled around and tried to bore a hole through his oily head with my eyes. "Get away from me."

"Ooooh, Kevie-Wevie is m-a-a-a-a-d," Stiller said. He laughed and gave me a shove. "Don't mess with me, prissy boy. I'll beat you 'til you wet your pants and beg for mercy." He moved closer, but I stood firm.

"Come on," he said. He shoved me again, this time knocking my books out of my arm. His face was red and sweat ran off his temples and down his cheeks. He was so close, I could smell his BO.

It was time to introduce him to the blacktop. I shoved him back. My face burned, my arms tensed, and my hands balled into tight fists. I knew I could whip him, and I was ready, but I'd make sure he was guilty of the first punch. I jammed my fists into my pockets, ready to release them at the first sign of assault. But there was something soft and squiggly in my right pocket—the fishing worm Herb Conrad had given me at Cletus McCulley's funeral. For a second my mind cleared, and my right fist relaxed. It was like someone opened the top of my head and let all the hot air out. Then two words entered my mind, as distinct as the ring when a crystal vase is tapped: *Walk away.*

My face must have gone blank, because Stiller stepped back and stared at me. "Wake up, Stupid," he yelled. "I want you paying attention when I beat the crap out of you!"

I heard the words again, just as clear as at first: *Walk away.* But why? I was bigger than Stiller, and I figured I was stronger, too. He'd be a big greasy spot on School Avenue by the time I finished with him. Then the voice came back once more, this time more forcefully: *Walk away, Kevin!*

I picked up my books. I didn't know why I should do it, but I knew what I had to do. I walked away. Stiller called after me, "You're afraid! You know I can ruin you! I'm not through with you, Kevin!"

I walked down the school drive and met Mom as she pulled in. I got in the truck and she asked if I was OK, because my face was red and I was sweating like crazy. I told her I was fine, and she didn't question me anymore about it.

The next day, Stiller was absent. And the next. Every day he was absent made me feel better, especially knowing I had Thanksgiving break—four more Stiller-free days—to look forward to. I also had something else to anticipate: Grandma and Granddad Kirk were stopping by on their way to Florida to spend the weekend with us—

and to celebrate my thirteenth birthday. I figured we'd all get a vacation, since I'd never heard of a funeral being held on Thanksgiving Day.

I was wrong.

When Mom picked me up after school on the day before Thanksgiving, she told me I'd have to help her get the chapel ready. Oda Mae Pidcock had passed away in her sleep. She was 104 years old. Her funeral would be Thanksgiving morning at ten. She wasn't a Latter-day Saint, but since the family had no church to call on, President Carter offered to do the funeral. Grandma and Granddad had already arrived for the weekend and had parked their RV in the back lot. Grandma would cook Thanksgiving dinner for us, so we would celebrate later in the day.

We pulled into the Paramount parking lot, and I could see Granddad's motor home parked in the grass behind the home. As Mom eased the S-10 into the garage, I saw my bird baths, disassembled and leaning against the back wall. Mom had moved them from the back lot before Granddad and Grandma arrived. Granddad wasn't very observant—she probably assumed he would run over them while trying to park the RV.

Grandma was waiting for me outside the door of the motor home. She'd been making pumpkin pies and the smell wafted out the screen door, wrapping around me like a hug before I'd even reached Grandma's outstretched arms.

"Sweetie," Grandma said as she draped her fleshy arms around my neck, "you've grown so much!"

I laughed. "So have you, Grandma."

Grandma pushed me back, looking me up and down the way grandmothers do to make sure you're healthy and still eating plenty. Dressed in orange sweats, she had a green scarf tied around her hair, making her look like a pear-shaped pumpkin. "Oh, poo. I've only gained a few pounds," she said, patting her hips. "Besides, grandmas are supposed to be soft and cuddly." She began shaking her backside to emphasize her point, and her entire body below the neck jiggled like the big pan of orange gelatin they'd set out for lunch that day in the school cafeteria.

Mom nudged me in the back with my backpack. "I've told you not to make comments about Grandma Kirk's weight."

"Oh Freda, don't be so uptight," Grandma said, and she giggled. "Kevin and I like to have a little fun with each other, don't we, Sweetie?" She turned her head to the side and gave me a big, open-mouthed wink.

I gave Grandma one right back and Mom let out a big sigh. "Since I'm the only one who thinks it's rude to discuss someone else's weight, I'll just take your backpack upstairs." She walked back toward the Paramount, dragging the backpack and shaking her head.

"So Grandma, how long can you and Granddad stay?"

"Just 'til the day after Thanksgiving, Sweetie," Grandma said. She held the door open for me to step inside the motor home. "We have reservations at a campground near Fort Walton Beach, and we can't be a day late or they'll sell our spot to someone else." She rummaged through a drawer underneath the built-in couch and pulled out a big brown envelope. She started to hand it to me, but Granddad opened the door.

"Where's my grandson?" Granddad stuck his head through the doorway and looked up and down the interior of the motor home, pretending like he couldn't see me. "I drive all the way to this ungodly Arkansas hole-in-the-wall to see my only grandson and he doesn't even stick around to greet his elderly grandfather who's already got one foot in the grave."

"Now Papa," Grandma said. "Armadillo is a quaint little town."

"Only if you can stomach running over the little buggers." Granddad loved to travel, but he also loved to find things to gripe about while traveling. Our town's namesake was giving him something to grouse about. "Armadillos, I mean. I think I hit at least three of 'em after I crossed the city limits. They crack like walnuts."

Grandma shuddered. "Hush, Papa. That sounds awful."

Granddad stretched his arms out and motioned to me for a hug. "It's the truth and you know it. They're speed bumps with legs. You hit one doing sixty-five and there goes your front end. Betcha I'll have to get it realigned before we get to Alabama."

I hugged him back, but didn't have to stretch to do it. Granddad wasn't much taller than Dad—but he did have a lot more hair, all of it a peppery gray, with a moustache to match. "Well, Granddad, I hate to disappoint you, but that's about the only excitement you'll find around here."

As it turned out, I was wrong about that, too.

Oda Mae Pidcock's family trickled in for the visitation Wednesday evening. She was so old that she must have outlived all of her friends and most of her family. This was the smallest group we'd had for a visitation so far. But they also turned out to be the rowdiest.

Ten minutes before closing, her grandsons gathered around the casket. From my spot at the door, I couldn't hear very well, but I could see their rough gestures. They were in heavy disagreement. One pointed to the casket, another to the body; one pointed to the door, another began shouting. I began to catch bits of the conversation, like, "This is mine," "That's mine," "I did this," and "She promised me." Then the shoving started, and just like that they were all over each other. I beeped Dad on the radio. He and President Carter were in the office together, planning the next day's service.

"Dad, there's a fight!"

Dad didn't answer. By this time the men were rolling on the floor, fists flying. One fell back and his head hit the front pew with a loud pop.

I beeped again. "DAD! GET UP HERE, NOW!"

Dad had heard the noise, and he and President Carter were already coming down the hall. The floor rattled and vibrated each time one of the cousins got knocked down. By the time Dad and President Carter made it halfway across the chapel, the casket stand was swaying back and forth, as if it were dodging the cousins' fists. I punched 911 on the cell phone and in less than two minutes we had blue lights flashing in the parking lot. It took four police officers to untangle the kicking cousins. They pulled them up from the floor, out of the fight, and arrested them all. One officer called central dispatch for extra backup, and I held the door as the screaming, handcuffed family was escorted to the waiting cruisers.

Dad got his toolbox out of the maintenance closet, and he and President Carter got to work tightening the bolts that were supposed to sturdy the casket stand. They looked like two auto mechanics, occasionally sliding out to exchange tools. I sat in the back of the chapel and listened.

"I should have expected this," Dad said in a muffled voice. "Freda said when she went to pick up the body, the family was arguing over that poor old woman's jewelry."

President Carter scooted out to get a bigger socket. "At least they didn't tip the casket," he said. He picked up several different sockets and inspected them, only to find none were the right size. "Arlice, have you got the five-eighths socket?"

"Sure," Dad said, handing it to him from under the stand. "Take this one and give me the three-sixteenths."

On Thanksgiving morning, the crowd for Oda Mae Pidcock's funeral was even smaller than the visitation because half of her living relatives were still in jail from the night before. President Carter offered a short sermon and the organist played an abbreviated version of "Amazing Grace." When what was left of the family filed by the casket for the final viewing, a large distraught woman threw herself on top of the open coffin. Her hair was dyed tomato red, and she had on so much cheap jewelry that I wondered how much change it had taken to empty out the Gum 'n Gems machine at the Cow Palace. She wailed over and over, "Nanny! Nanny! Oh, dear Lord! Give me back my Nanny!"

President Carter leaned over to console her and was thanked by getting her arm, which was about the size of a tree trunk, whacked across his chest. President Carter staggered back and caught himself on the edge of the pew before he totally lost balance. With an arm like that, I figured she must have been the one to teach all her cousins how to fight.

The more the tomato-haired lady rocked back and forth, the more the casket, and the stand, rocked back and forth too. That squealing-tires sound slipped up from Mom's throat.

"Arrrrrrlice," she screeched, "do something!"

Dad dashed down the aisle as dignified as one could dash in a suit and in the middle of a funeral chapel. He reached for Tomato Lady, hoping to back her away from the casket, but he was too late. The stand tilted and the whole enchilada hit the floor with a sickening thud. Every flower arrangement on the right side of the room somersaulted through the air. The casket tipped over on its side, and poor Oda Mae Pidcock was dumped unceremoniously onto the floor.

Tomato Lady fainted. Mom and Dad stuffed Oda Mae back into her box, then they helped the paramedics haul Tomato Lady out to the ambulance.

That afternoon, we ate Thanksgiving dinner in the motor home with Granddad and Grandma Kirk—turkey, gravy, dressing, mashed potatoes, the works. By the time evening rolled around, I'd finished off an entire pumpkin pie by myself. Mom was in bed by seven with a terrific headache. I don't know if it was caused by the funeral or the jokes Dad and Granddad cracked about it all through dinner. The worst was when Granddad said he knew a good pharmacist if Mom needed something to "stop her coffin."

While Dad and Granddad cleaned up the Thanksgiving dishes that night, I took Grandma out behind the motor home to show her where I liked to sit and record animal sightings. She was impressed and told me she'd take lots of pictures of the wildlife at Fort Walton Beach and send them to me. The only wildlife I could imagine at a campground full of retired people would be the Saturday night bingo crowd. So I smiled and told her I'd like that a lot. Then she pulled a big brown envelope out of her jacket. It was the envelope she'd tried to give me earlier.

"Kevin, I want to give you this," Grandma said, and placed the envelope in my hands. "I hope to be able to give you more sometime, but this is all I have right now."

I opened the envelope and pulled the papers out. They looked like charts, but I had no idea what they were for.

Grandma pointed to the first name on the top sheet. "This is a pedigree chart. This is you, and this is your family tree." She let her fingers trace along the brackets. "This is Arlice, and your granddad, and your great-granddad, and your great-great-granddad. And below there's me, your great-grandma, and your great-great grandma." She slid the papers back in the envelope, bent the clasp, and put the envelope in my hands.

"Thanks, Grandma." I didn't understand why she'd want to give me stuff like this, but I didn't want to sound ungrateful.

"Granddad and I aren't getting any younger, Kevin," Grandma said. She gazed out beyond the trees. "Someday we won't be around anymore."

"Don't talk like that, Grandma."

"It's true, Sweetie. Not talking about it won't make the truth go away. Over the last few months, I've been researching our family history. I'm recording as much as I can remember about all the old family stories. If I don't write them down, they'll be forgotten. People will be forgotten." She caressed my cheek with her wrinkled hand. It was warm and soft, her skin paper thin. "And Kevin, a grandma doesn't want to think that she'll be forgotten."

I let Grandma pull me in for a hug. I didn't say anything because I felt a sharp pain in my stomach and was afraid if I opened my mouth, the only thing to come out would be a squeak—or worse, a sob. Instead, I concentrated real hard, and wished Grandma could hear what was in my mind.

I will never forget you, Grandma. Or Granddad. I promise.

We heard a slight rustle a few feet away. Armadillos! Their clumsy, armored bodies looked like soldiers' helmets with legs and snouts. They scampered in and out of the trees. It was the first time I'd seen live armadillos since we'd moved to Armadillo.

"You guys had better not be here in the morning if you don't want to end up like your cousins," Grandma said. The armadillos stopped their game of tag and studied her. I wondered what they thought about this orange, pumpkin-shaped human who was trying to give them advice.

We tried intimidating them by staring them down, but Grandma got tickled and let out a loud snort. The armadillos turned their backs to us and retreated into the safety of the trees, their pointy tails dragging through the brittle autumn leaves.

Chapter Eleven

Stiller came back to school after Thanksgiving break with a broken arm. He was always coming to school bruised up. Since he never stopped looking for a fight, I figured the bruises meant he wasn't having trouble finding one.

He still hated my guts, but he stopped his verbal attacks against me for a while. As long as I kept plenty of space between us, I could avoid getting tripped, shoved, or spit on. And I covered the books in my locker with sheets of plastic wrap. That kept my stuff from getting gunky when he used my locker for a trash can.

I puzzled a lot over what happened that day when Stiller wanted to beat me up after school. I'd never felt rage like that before, and I wasn't proud of myself for it. I wanted to believe my anger was justified, that I had every right in the world to break his skull open. But something kept nagging at me, telling me that forcing him to kiss the concrete would not resolve the problem.

I've never believed in rabbit's feet, lucky coins, or four-leaf clovers. But when I touched that purple plastic fishing worm, it distracted me enough to make me think twice about annihilating Stiller. I'd kept that worm in my pocket since Cletus McCulley's funeral. I wasn't sure why. Herb Conrad said that he and Cletus always carried bait in their pockets. But it was December, too cold to fish, and I still couldn't leave for school in the mornings without checking to make sure I hadn't forgotten the worm.

Why was I carrying something that helped me remember a dead man, a man I'd never met while he was alive? I could see his face in my mind, as clear as in the portrait that stood beside his casket. And I couldn't forget the dream I'd had about him.

That dream had seemed so real. I'd read his thoughts as clear as if he'd been speaking, but I didn't hear his voice—not until he looked at me and said, "There's more to life than what you see." How could something—or someone—be living if you couldn't see it living? I understood that things like electricity or radio waves or wind couldn't be seen but still existed. Once the graveyard became your permanent address, though, you were out to lunch for good. Right?

The first week of December, Mom decorated the funeral home for Christmas. When she brought up the idea, Dad winced and I told her that happy blinking lights and snowmen would look weird in a funeral home. And you sure couldn't have any life-size replicas of the Big Red Guy. All it would take would be for one little kid to see a stiff Santa lying in repose at the Paramount, and all residents of Sherman County less than eight years old would be traumatized for life.

Fortunately, the effect Mom had in mind was peaceful and dignified instead of mistletoe and ho-ho-ho. She set up a tall artificial tree in the front hall and covered it in white midget lights, doves, satin balls, and plastic icicle ornaments. Then she draped garlands of gold beads on the branch tips and surrounded the base with pots of red and white poinsettias. Outside the front entrance, she wrapped pine boughs around the columns and encircled them with more poinsettias. Upstairs, in the living area, we had our old tree with all the ornaments I'd made in kindergarten, grade school, and Cub Scouts, finished off with the twinkle lights that flashed like the multi-colored sign over the Cow Palace.

Business was too good. We were doing three funerals a week, and it was hard for Mom and Dad to keep up with everything. Even during the breaks between services, there were still chores to be done, supplies to buy, and the upstairs to care for. And Dad had been warning Mom since early fall that the public restrooms would have to be renovated in the spring. They tossed around the idea of bringing in an apprentice, but they couldn't afford to do that until after the first of the year. So when school let out for Christmas break, Mom greeted me with a list of major jobs. Within a few days we were able to finish all the big tasks, which gave us a chance to get our Christmas shopping done in time for the holidays.

Christmas Eve and Christmas Day were quiet. I got up early both mornings and sat out in the back lot. Snow covered the ground, making it easy to see rabbit, deer, and bird tracks. I drew pictures of them in my notebook. I liked to call my notebooks volumes, and the current one was Volume IV. Sometimes I fantasized about finding a new subspecies and getting an award from the National Geographic Society. My name would be in all the scientific journals as Kevin Kirk, the bright young amateur biologist who discovered what for years more experienced researchers had been looking for. Mom and Dad were impressed with my hobby—so impressed that they gave me a pair of binoculars and some books on animal, plant, and insect identification for Christmas.

The day after Christmas, Dad went to the hospital to pick up a body while Mom and I hit the post-holiday sales. When we got home, I went upstairs to my room and Mom went downstairs to help Dad. I messed around on the computer, flipped through my new books, and before I knew it, I'd fallen asleep—rare for me, because I never take naps. I woke up about six. Mom and Dad still hadn't come upstairs. It was odd for both of them to be downstairs for this long without taking a break.

I went to the refrigerator and took a swig of orange juice—out of the jug, since I was by myself—to take the taste of sleep out of my mouth. There was a note on the table from Mom:

> *Arlice,*
>
> *Gone to Wal-Mart. I forgot to buy more panty hose.*
>
> *Be right back.*
>
> *Love u, Freda*

I went downstairs to look for Dad and found him in the chapel. He was standing beside a small blue casket, and he was crying.

I had never seen my father cry.

I stepped back quietly and slipped upstairs. I'd seen Dad act goofy, mad, worried, and frustrated, but I'd never heard him sob as if his heart were breaking. It was an unfamiliar, frightening sound, like the sickening pop when two cars collide.

That night after my parents were asleep, I snuck down to the chapel. I flipped on the front lights and walked up to the casket. I lifted the lid and inside, nestled in the palest blue satin, was the body of a baby girl.

She couldn't have been more than three months old. She wore a white cotton gown spotted with white satin rosebuds, a white lace cap on her head, and white knit booties on her feet. Inside the lid of the casket, someone had pinned a blue card to the lining. The baby's name, Gretchen, was on the card, written in calligraphy. And below that, the definition: "Little Pearl."

At first glance, Gretchen would have appeared to be more at home on a toy store shelf, peek-a-booing through the clear plastic window of a cheerfully colored cardboard box. But she had once been a living child; her body was definitely flesh, not plastic. I touched the tip of my finger to her forehead, in the same spot where her mother and father had probably kissed her many times. Then it would have been warm and soft. Now it was cool and lifeless, unresponsive to contact.

All the funerals we'd had at the Paramount so far were for people who had lived so long their bodies wore out from years and years of use. But this was a baby—a new body, a new life, a new promise. It didn't seem fair. Gretchen had died before she was even old enough to learn to say Mommy or Daddy. Before she could learn to read or write. Before she could learn how to cross the street alone or ride a bike. Before she could go to school, win a spelling bee, hit a home run, drive a car, graduate from college. Before she could marry and have a baby of her own.

A blanket of sadness draped over my chest. I could understand why Dad had been so distressed. I wondered about Mom's reaction.

I slowly lowered the lid, shut off the lights, and left the chapel. I eased the double doors closed and started down the hall to the stairs.

"What are you doing, Kevin?"

I'd been caught. The light was off in the guest kitchen, but Mom was in there. She popped the top on a can of diet soda and poured it over a glass of ice. How long had she been down here? She was wearing a pair of Dad's old sweats and a Habitat for Humanity T-shirt. Her furry frog slippers stared at me from under the table. "I thought you didn't like having dead bodies in the house at night."

"I couldn't sleep." Well, at least it wasn't a lie.

"Grab a drink and sit down," she gestured to the chair across from her. "There's some ice in the freezer. And hit the light switch."

I turned on the light, then got the key from the cabinet and opened the vending machine. There was one cold root beer, so I sat down and drank it straight from the can. I was halfway through when Mom finally spoke.

"I saw you touch the baby."

"Yeah."

"I thought you didn't want to have anything to do with the bodies."

I remembered Dad's promise before we moved, that I'd never have to touch a dead body. He'd said it in a joking way, but here I'd just gone and touched one without anyone making me do it. "I don't know," I said. I studied my can so I wouldn't have to look at Mom. "It seemed like . . . well, it doesn't seem right for a baby to be dead like that. She was only a baby. I could see why Dad was so upset."

Mom raised her eyebrows. "Your father was upset?"

I wished I hadn't said anything. "Well, yeah, a little. I mean, well, I saw him earlier and he seemed kind of sad."

"How sad?"

"He was crying."

"Crying," Mom echoed, her voice flat. The color drained from her skin, like it does when you have the flu and you're just about to throw up.

"Well, more like bawling, actually. Sobbing, really."

Mom put her elbows on the table and dropped her face into her hands. She was quiet for a minute, and then she looked up to the ceiling, like Dad did when we had our talk at the Cow Palace. "Oh Arlice," she said. "Why didn't you tell me?"

I got up to go to bed. This funeral home business was making us all crazy: me hearing voices and carrying a worm in my pocket to remind me of a dead man, Dad crying over somebody else's dead baby, and Mom talking to the ceiling. Maybe we could still get out of the Paramount and go back to the way things used to be, back before Stiller and moving and living with death every day. Back to when the toughest thing to digest was Mom's cooking.

Mom looked down at the table and shook her head. "It's Kelsey. He's still upset about Kelsey."

"The baby's name was Gretchen, Mom," I said over my shoulder as I started out the door.

"I'm not talking about the baby in the chapel, Kevin. I'm talking about Kelsey. She was your sister."

Chapter Twelve

I just stood there in the doorway for what seemed like an eternity, my body frozen smack in the middle of the motion of walking away.

"I think you should know about your sister, Kev," Mom said. Her voice was low and quivery. "Come back and sit down."

Even my mouth felt numb. "OK."

Mom grabbed a napkin from the holder on the table and dabbed her eyes. "About five years before you were born, I was pregnant with our first child. Everything seemed fine—no problems or complications. But the umbilical cord wrapped around her neck during labor. The doctor didn't know it until it was too late. She was born dead."

Mom dabbed her eyes again. "She was so perfect—her fingers and toes, her tiny ringlets of black hair—but she was dead. People said, 'Don't take it so hard. You can have another one.' But how could there be another Kelsey?

"Arlice had just finished his apprenticeship at Barre Family Mortuary. They had offered him a chance to become a partner in the business. Everything seemed to be going so perfect for us. He had the promise of steady work; we were starting a family—a family we hoped would last forever. We never dreamed anything would go wrong. We had Kelsey's nursery ready and a closet full of little dresses and diapers just waiting for her. But she died. After that, Arlice quit his job at the mortuary and went to the factory."

A closet full of little dresses.

I remembered the shoebox—the one I'd found when we were packing. Mom had yelled at me because she thought I was going to throw it away. It had a white cotton dress with white silk rosebuds in it. And a white lace cap. And white knit booties. Those weren't doll clothes. Those were Kelsey's clothes.

"Remember when we packed and you screamed at me over that shoebox?"

"Yes, that was Kelsey's dress. We were going to have her blessed in it."

Gretchen was wearing the same kind of dress. Then I had a thought so bizarre I was sure Mom would say I was wrong. "You put Kelsey's dress on Gretchen, didn't you?"

"Yes, I dressed that baby in Kelsey's clothes."

I stared at Mom in disbelief. "You yelled at me because I was going to throw away the dress, but if you decide to bury it in the ground that's OK?"

"Kevin, Gretchen's parents don't even have enough money to pay us. I can't turn them away. They don't even have a decent dress to bury Gretchen in. Kelsey's dress isn't doing anyone any good hidden in the closet. Besides, I think this could help us put the past where it belongs."

"You think the past should be buried? Well, I don't think it's working. The way Dad was bawling, it's not working for him, either." I should have felt sorry for my parents. Instead, I was mad. "Why did you hide this from me?"

"We never meant to hide it, Kev," Mom said. "But it's hard to talk about. What hurts me most of all is that your father blames God for what happened. He says if God was as loving as the Church says He is, He would have never taken Kelsey away from us."

This was the first time I'd ever heard either of my parents mention God or church when discussing our family. "When did you guys ever go to church? You've never taken me to church."

"Shortly after we married, we met some missionaries. I had just become pregnant, and we were thrilled to find a church that taught families could be together not just on earth, but in heaven too."

She paused. "We're Mormons, Kev."

I couldn't believe my parents had, in all the years of my life, never, ever, not even once mentioned any of this. I'd been lied to again, just like when they didn't tell me the whole story about the funeral home. Except this time it was worse, much worse. Now I questioned whether I really even knew my family at all. I got up to throw away my root beer can, but instead I threw it across the room.

"How can I believe anything you say to me, Mom? How many other major events have you avoided telling me about just because you thought I was a kid and didn't need to know?"

I heard a sniff or two, then a full-blown sob. Mom dropped her head down on the table. She cried so hard the whole table wobbled.

Then I recalled the look on Dad's face the night Mom casually mentioned President Carter's offer to conduct funerals, and how she tried to make the offer sound as if it were no big deal.

"Now I know why Dad acted so funny when you told him President Carter wanted to help. You want Dad to have contact with the Church again. Is that why you agreed to let President Carter help? Or was it your idea, and you approached President Carter about it, hoping Dad would talk to someone about what happened?"

I gave Mom a moment to answer, but she didn't. She just kept on sobbing. I turned my back to her. "I'm going back to bed."

"Kevin, please wait," Mom called out. "Let me finish."

I didn't want to be in the same room with her, and I was so mad I wanted to punch the wall. Even though she couldn't quit sniffling, I didn't feel sorry for her. Yet I stopped just short of the door. I guess I hoped she would say something that would help me make sense of the whole thing.

Mom hiccupped. She took a deep breath to control her tears, then continued. "After Kelsey died, your dad said he'd lost his job. But Mr. Barre told me later that Arlice had quit. When I confronted him about it, I realized he'd quit because of Kelsey. His job was to help families deal with death, but he didn't know how to deal with it himself. He wasn't prepared for the emotions we felt when Kelsey died."

If Kelsey had lived, I thought, *she'd be eighteen now. She'd probably have long black hair and eyes like Mom's.* "What made Dad agree to buy the Paramount, then?"

"I talked him into it. We needed to start a business. I knew this was our best chance. I thought—I hoped—enough time had gone by. And Arlice was never happy at the factory. He needs to work where he's at his best, where he can care for others.

"Kevin, it would mean more to me than anything if your dad would soften his heart toward the Church. I know it's not God's fault that Kelsey died. I also know your dad still believes in God. But until he finds a way to cope with his grief, he'll continue to stay away."

"I can't believe you never told me about this."

"I'm sorry, Kevin."

"Sorry doesn't help, Mom," I said. I pushed the door open. "I don't understand why you couldn't tell me this. I've had a sister all along and never knew it."

"But she's dead."

"So? What did you say about Dad's Aunt Juanita? You forgot that she was dead because you loved her so much, remember? So it's OK to talk about Aunt Juanita but it's not OK to talk about Kelsey? Not even to tell me about her?"

Mom choked on a sob. "It's so hard, Kevin. You wouldn't understand. We just couldn't bring ourselves to talk about it."

"You don't know that I wouldn't understand," I shot back, so angry now that my stomach cramped and the veins in my neck throbbed. "You never give me the chance to understand anything!"

Mom shrunk down in the seat. "I didn't know losing a child could still hurt after so long."

I left my mother sitting at the table, alone, and went back to my room.

I crawled in bed and yanked the covers over my head, hoping the blackness would swallow me up and I could sleep. Instead, I rolled in the dark for a long time. I had a sister. A sister I never knew.

If I didn't know her, why did it hurt so bad?

When I woke up the next morning, I found a paper on my nightstand. It was Kelsey's birth certificate. Kelsey Lizabeth Kirk. Six pounds, eight and one-half ounces. Eighteen inches long. Her birth and death date were listed as the same day, with a tiny set of footprints like exclamation points underneath as if to say, I was here!

The goose bumps I got from Cletus McCulley's words erupted again.

There's more to life than what you see.

There was no funeral for baby Gretchen. Her parents followed us to the cemetery in a beat-up station wagon. Her plot was in the far west corner, her tiny grave marked by a small piece of polished granite no wider across than a dinner plate. I found out later that it had taken all the money the couple had to buy the baby's plot and headstone. My parents had not only dressed and buried Gretchen at no charge, but gave her parents some money to help them get back to their family in Texas.

Late that afternoon, I sat out in the back lot with my new binoculars. The wind was light but cold. Powdered-sugar snow floated down from the gray sky, clung to the evergreens, and spread across the ground like vanilla frosting. There were no animals out, just an occasional bird, so I filled up the last page of Volume IV with observations about the trees.

Using my new binoculars, I focused on a distant pine branch that had two cones hanging underneath. I mentally traced the outlines of the needles, the cones, and the downy snow as it piled on top. Though hundreds of feet away, I felt close enough to the branch to touch its smallest needle.

I studied that branch for so long that my elbows stiffened and my fingers froze into an icy grip on the binoculars. I lowered them and saw the sky had descended into a deep lavender haze. The single branch I'd studied was now lost, now one of many secrets hidden within the shadows of the trees.

I gathered my stuff and went back to my room. I stacked the newly completed Volume IV on top of Volumes III, II, and I. I pulled a new notebook out of my desk, wrote Volume V on the cover, and promoted it to its new place among my research supplies. Then I took my photo album off the shelf. I stretched out across the bed and began flipping through the pages of me as a baby, then a toddler, then a preschooler. Mom, or Dad, or both, were in every picture. Then there were school pictures and class pictures, pictures with my old friends outside my old house, pictures of birthday parties and Halloween parties and Christmases at Grandma Kirk's.

I remembered the envelope Grandma had given me on Thanksgiving. I pulled the trunk of junk from under my bed and began rummaging. The envelope was buried underneath my box of old baseball cards and the bag of one hundred fifty plastic insects I'd bought at the Dollar Store when I was in second grade. I pulled out the papers. The first one was a pedigree chart. My name was number one, Kevin Andrew Kirk. Dad's name was number two: Arlice Theobald Kirk. Yuck! Any parent who would name his son Theobald might as well slap a Kick Me sign on the kid's back. A name like that is an open invitation to get pummeled by guys like Stiller.

Granddad was number three: James Theobald Kirk. I'd always thought it was cool to have a grandfather named James T. Kirk. Dad told me once that when he was in elementary school, he always made sure Granddad was the one who signed his report cards. He'd take them back to school and show the signature to his friends. Because his family moved around so much, Dad always told his new classmates his father was in a top secret army space program. Once his friends saw Granddad's signature, Dad never confirmed—or denied—the rumors that his dad was the captain of the starship *Enterprise*.

I picked up Kelsey's birth certificate—Kelsey Lizabeth Kirk, daughter of Arlice Theobald Kirk and Freda Jean Killough. I laid it on top of Grandma's papers and slid them all into the envelope, bent the clasp back into place, and put it back in my trunk in its spot underneath the baseball cards.

I got up and walked to the window. Now it was dark, but the sky had cleared and the moon was full. The snow-covered pine boughs sparkled, competing with the stars overhead. The soft sounds of my parents' conversation drifted up from the den and through the slightly open door. I could see them sitting on opposite ends of the couch, legs stretched out, Mom's resting on top of Dad's. They were totally focused on each other.

I flopped back on the bed and pulled the fishing worm out of my pocket. I held it up to the light and the silver specks in it glittered like the snow outside. I thought about Kelsey as I twirled it around in my fingers. I wondered how the worm would look to a fish if he saw it hanging from a hook in the middle of a big lake. How could he see it floating in front of him if his eyes were in the sides of his head?

An artist visited our school once. He painted old barns and snow-topped mountains, log cabins, and whitewashed country churches nestled in autumn leaves. Someone asked how he knew the colors and shapes would end up like the scene he had in mind. He said that as he worked, he liked to step back from his paintings and observe them from across the room. If you're always in the same spot, always too close, he said, you can't see how the shapes, the light, and the shadows blend together. Sometimes you have to back up to see how each element becomes part of the whole picture.

I put the worm on my desk and changed into my pajamas. I brushed my teeth, then as I washed my hands I looked at myself in the mirror, moving my face so close to it that my breath fogged the glass. I could have counted each eyelash if I'd wanted to. Then I slowly backed away and watched my cheeks, chin, forehead, ears, and hair all come together to make my face. A few more backward steps and my surroundings—the shower curtain, shelves, and seashell wallpaper—came into view, telling the story of where I was at that moment.

Mom's giggle made its way from the den to my ears, interrupting my concentration. "Oh Arlice," she teased, "you're so kooky." Dad's familiar cackle followed, which meant he'd zinged Mom with one of his corny one-liners.

Isn't it funny how you can live with your parents for so long and not really know them at all?

Chapter Thirteen

We started out the new year with a new apprentice. The Paramount was getting to be too much for Mom and Dad to handle alone, so Marcy moved into the small efficiency apartment above the hearse garage. She was finishing her degree at the same school Mom had attended. The home she worked at was closing, so she needed to find an apprentice position somewhere else.

Marcy was the kind of person who didn't just arrive somewhere—she made an entrance. It wasn't because Marcy was arrogant—in fact, she was so unpretentious you felt like she'd enjoy a barn dance as much as the Metropolitan Opera. She was born elegant, the same way some people are born with perfect teeth.

On the day she came for her interview, she wore a tailored wool suit with matching pink pumps. She flowed through the front door like a pale pink breeze, her long slender braids brushing across her shoulders as she glided down the hall to the office. I'd never seen anyone with such excellent posture. I wondered if she was the descendant of an African queen.

I liked Marcy from the minute she shook my hand, which she did as if I were twenty-six, like her. Mom was even more impressed with Marcy. Her fifteen-minute interview ended up taking three hours. When Dad came home from running errands in town, he and Mom spent another two hours in the office with Marcy. Afterward, Dad took us all to the Cow Palace to celebrate the hiring of the Paramount's new apprentice.

I'd heard people talk about starving college students. Marcy must have been famished. She inhaled two Bacon and Cheese Double Cow Patties, an order of Onion Lassos, a side salad with extra ranch dressing, and three soda refills. Marcy was built like a beanpole, but she could eat enough to feed the entire Sherman

County High football team, plus the mascot. By the time she'd scraped the last bit of hot fudge brownie sundae from her plate, she was calling Mom and Dad "Mr. and Mrs. K," and the three acted like they'd known each other forever.

Marcy was also athletic, which explained why her back was as straight as a ruler. Every weekday she was up at 5:30 A.M. for a three-mile run, and every other day she did a thirty-minute workout with free weights. I found this out when I went out to the back lot one morning shortly after she'd moved in. The lights were on in the hearse garage, and when I peeked in the window, there was Marcy doing chin-ups on a bar hanging from the ceiling. I'd never seen anyone do so many chin-ups before.

She saw me and let go of the bar. "Come on in."

I opened the side door and stepped in. A Tina Turner CD played low in the background.

"Do you lift weights, Kevin?"

I didn't even think I could do a chin-up.

"I love lifting weights." Marcy exhaled and sat down on the bench, wiping the sweat from her forehead with an old towel. "Makes me feel like I can do anything. Try it." She handed me a dumbbell. "I'll show you how to do a bicep curl. Sit on the bench and support your elbow on this pad. Extend your arm and pull the weight up toward your shoulder. See?" She put her hand on my bicep and squeezed. "You can feel your muscle working."

I tried a bicep curl with my other arm. Marcy then asked if I wanted to try chin-ups. She picked me up just enough so I could grab the bar, then she let go. I dangled in the air, the tips of my toes nowhere near the concrete floor.

"Pull up with your biceps," she encouraged. I strained, feeling the muscles tingle as I pulled my weight up. "Pull . . . pull . . . pull . . . that's it!" She clapped and jumped when my chin went over for the first time. "Now lower yourself slowly . . . now pull up again . . ."

Dad came in just as my chin made it over the second time. "Look, Mr. K. Kevin's done two chin-ups!"

Dad gave Marcy a high five. "Way to go! You may put some muscles on this kid yet."

"My father used to lift weights," Marcy said. "That's how I learned to count when I was little. I helped him count his reps."

I let go of the bar. "He doesn't lift anymore?"

"He was killed by a drunk driver when I was eight," Marcy said. "On his way home from work."

Dad put his arm around Marcy's shoulder. "I'm so sorry, Marcy."

"My daddy was a good person. I miss him so much, even now."

That afternoon Dad bought an extra set of weights and a rowing machine to add to Marcy's makeshift gym, which surprised me since he was always worried about money. But Mom was thrilled because Marcy cried and thanked them over and over again, saying she knew she'd love working for them and buying that equipment made her feel like she'd found a home instead of a job. Soon we were all working out, and Marcy became our personal trainer. By the middle of the month I could do five chin-ups, which made me feel like I could handle five Stillers if I had to.

One night, while Mom and Dad were out on a date, Marcy challenged me to a game of Go Fish in the guest kitchen. I'd just put down my first set when there was a knock at the French doors leading out to the sitting area. A tall, flabby man in an overcoat had his face pressed to the glass. He waved, trying to get our attention. The last time I'd ever seen anything so pathetic was at the big pet store in the mall at Memphis, where the puppies peered out at you from behind bars with hopeful, yet pitiful, expressions.

Marcy groaned and threw her cards down. She got up and, instead of her usual grace, shuffled to the door on weighted feet.

"Marshall, what are you doing here?"

"I had to see you, Marcy. We have to talk."

"There's nothing to talk about," Marcy said. "I told you I need more time."

Marshall reached over and put his hands on her shoulders. "But baby, I love you. I've known it from the first time I heard you say my name. I want to spend the rest of my life with you. Please don't turn me away again."

"Marshall, this is Kevin." She tilted her

head toward me, her hands perched on her narrow hips. "I work for his parents."

"Hey." Marshall nodded, and then resumed his quest for true love. "Marcy, I promise if you'll just listen to me, if you'll just be reasonable—"

"Reasonable? Me, be reasonable? You're the one who needs to be reasonable!" She stepped back and Marshall's arms fell to his sides. He shrunk at least a foot and his shoulders drooped, making his already-round waistline even rounder. I heard a button on the front of his coat pop from the strain. His black eyes searched her face for any sign of compromise.

Marcy stood, her arms crossed, for what seemed like hours. Then she sighed. "OK. Tomorrow night. Pick me up at eight. You can take me out to dinner, and then you can tell me what's on your mind. But I refuse to listen to anything you have to say right now."

"But Marcy—"

"Good night, Marshall." She sat down and asked if I had any eights. Marshall stared at her for a minute, and then slouched his way back to the doors. He'd been dismissed. So like any guy guilty of the third out in the bottom of the ninth, he walked away—alone—into the cold, cold night.

The door clicked shut. "He doesn't know what he wants." She jerked the eights from my hand, put them with hers to make a set, and slapped them down on the table. She turned to the ceiling. "What does he want?" she said to the fluorescent light, as if it had all the answers and wasn't sharing any with her. Now I understood why she got along so well with my parents, since they talked to ceilings too. Or maybe it was just another quirky mortician's habit?

"Sounds to me like he wants to marry you," I said. I tried to sneak a peek at her cards. She'd relaxed her hand just enough for me to see the numbers at the top.

Marcy jerked her cards to her chest. "Stop peeking at my cards, you little cheat! Tryin' to catch me off guard?" She cocked her left eyebrow and studied me, her black eyes squinting to the size of slivered almonds. "And how would you know enough about Marshall Cartwright to give me any kind of opinion?"

"I've got ears. He said he loved you. And when someone says he wants to spend the rest of his life with you, you don't have to have an IQ of 150 to figure out what he means."

Marcy's frown stretched into a playful grin. "So when it comes to love, you're the answer man. And what makes you think you're qualified to give advice? You got a girlfriend?"

Immediately Dani's face popped in my mind and my cheeks began to burn. I said no, but it was overdone and sputtery, like when you're saying something you don't really mean.

Marcy reached over and pinched my cheek. "Don't worry, Kevin. I won't tell. But I'll bet she's cute."

"Dani's not my girlfriend," I said, hoping I sounded forceful. But Marcy's laugh meant she didn't believe me. "She's just my friend. The only real friend I have in school right now."

"Well, everyone needs a friend." Her eyes lingered on the doors. She was quiet for a moment. When she spoke again the words strung out long and soft like spider's silk. "It's scary to admit to someone that he's all you think about all the time. What if my feelings are wrong? What if he's not the one?"

Then she fanned out the cards in her hand, and released a question as if it were a weight too heavy for her to lift: "But what if he is . . . and I lose him?"

Chapter Fourteen

By the end of January, we all knew Marshall Cartwright. He was at the Paramount almost every day, doing anything he could to be close to Marcy. When Dad remodeled the women's rest room, Marshall was there every afternoon after work. He helped Dad replace the old tile, install the new toilets, and hook up the new double sink. When Mom cleaned the carpets, Marshall was there to move the furniture. He even picked me up from school a couple of times when Mom was tied up. And like Marcy, he began calling Mom and Dad "Mr. and Mrs. K."

I got the feeling that Marcy didn't have much of a family. I never heard her talk about her mother, and after the day she taught me how to do chin-ups she never mentioned her father again. But it didn't take long for us to become her substitute family. If she and Marshall were going out, she checked with my parents first to make sure it didn't conflict with their schedule. Mom and Dad worried if she stayed out late, so Marcy always called to let them know when she came in. And Marcy loved to tease me. I didn't mind. In fact, I liked to think that if Kelsey had lived, she would have been a lot like Marcy.

It seemed odd that Marcy ended up at the Paramount right after Mom told me the truth about Kelsey. So I began to wonder: Could God have led Marcy to our family? I'd never given much thought to who God was or what He was up to. Mom had never mentioned anything about God—or going to church—until that night in the guest kitchen. Dad had never talked about Him before, so why should I?

But I couldn't deny that something about our family changed when Marcy came along, and the only explanation I could think of was that it was all God's doing. President Carter had said during Cletus McCulley's funeral service that when God gives us blessings, those blessings often come through other people. It didn't make sense to me then, but it did now. Maybe God thought my parents needed Marcy, and that Marcy needed them. It made me feel good inside to think God was actually concerned about my family—even though Dad was mad at Him.

The week before Valentine's, I went to the Bowlin' Hole with Marcy and Marshall. We bowled three games and ate chili dogs with cheese, and hot fudge sundaes. When Marshall got up to refill his soda at the self-serve fountain, I caught Marcy watching him. Her eyes were soft and round, her lips turned up slightly at the corners—the same way I'd seen Mom do when Dad used to come home from work in the afternoons. But the second Marshall turned around the look vanished.

I thought about that look during lunch later that week as I sat with Dani. She wasn't my girlfriend, but I sure did like her a lot. And she was pretty. Not like a model, just pretty in a way all her own. Pretty because of the kind of person she was inside.

I didn't realize I was staring at her until she caught me. My cheeks burned and as I tried to focus on tearing my string cheese, I hoped I hadn't been staring at her for too long. The silence was awkward, so I started a conversation.

"I think you were right about Stiller," I said. "I'm not so new anymore, so I guess he got tired of me."

Dani took a sip from her juice box. "We all know how he is. We've gone to school together for years. I've heard there's a new guy in 702 that he's picking on. But have you also noticed Chuck's been absent one or two days every week since he broke his arm?"

"So?"

Dani exhaled. It was a cute, exasperated little huff. "Maybe he has a problem."

"Who cares," I said, gnawing on my beef jerky, "as long as he leaves me alone."

"I guess I just feel sorry for him."

"Sorry? Why feel sorry for him? If you want to feel sorry for anybody, feel sorry for the ones he threatens and beats up on." Where were her loyalties, anyway? "Why feel sorry for someone who'd just as soon knock out your teeth as look at you? The way I see it, if he has a problem, he deserves whatever he gets and more."

Dani's brown eyes narrowed behind her glasses. "Kevin Kirk," she said, pronouncing the Ks slowly and deliberately, "I am disappointed in you. I thought you were more compassionate than that."

For just a second, my pride was hurt. Then I thought, *Who does she think she is, telling me she's disappointed in me?* I gritted my teeth. "And why am I supposed to feel compassion for this snot-wad who wants to kick my butt? Maybe I should go up to him and say, 'I know you're having problems, Stiller, so abuse me all you want to?' How about if I offer to let him beat me up when he's having a bad day? Would that make you happy?"

Dani got up, dumped her tray, and didn't speak to me the rest of the day. I tried calling her on the phone that night, but her mother said she had homework and couldn't talk.

The next morning I was at my locker and got the feeling that someone was standing behind me. It was Stiller. His right jaw was swollen and blue.

"I haven't forgotten about you, Kannibal. I'm always watching you, your every move."

I finished organizing my books and closed my locker. But Stiller didn't like to be ignored. He grabbed my chin and yanked my face around. I was so close I could see the dirty pores on his nose. I reached up and knocked his hand away.

Then I heard Mrs. Goldwyn's soft, familiar voice—except this time it was deepened by authority. "Good morning, boys."

Stiller suddenly turned polite. "We were just talking about Kevin's project for science class."

"I'm glad to see you two are getting along so well. Say hello to your parents for me, Kevin."

"Yes ma'am."

As soon as Mrs. Goldwyn turned the corner, I told Stiller to stay away from me. He laughed and took off down the hall. I felt something wet on the front of my shirt. I rubbed my hand on my chest and realized he'd squirted ink all over me.

Regardless of what Dani thought, I couldn't let him push me around anymore. I was ready to put him out of business. So when school let out, I went looking for Stiller. I told him to meet me behind the stadium—alone.

It was cold, and as I waited for Stiller to show up my mind felt as heavy as the fat, gray clouds overhead. I didn't want to admit it, but part of me hoped he would chicken out. Something in my chest hurt, like when you feel sorry for something you've done. But I hadn't done anything yet.

All it took was seeing Stiller round the corner to remind me why I was there: the ink on my shirt, the threats in class, the embarrassment in front of Dani and everyone else. The hurt in my chest turned to anger.. And that anger made me want to hurt Stiller, so he'd know how badly he'd hurt me.

But just as Stiller stopped a few feet in front of me, Marshall's red Honda turned into the gravel lot behind the stadium.

Marshall rolled down his window. "Kevin, I'm supposed to give you a ride home."

Stiller stared at me so hard his eyes didn't even blink.

"Am I interrupting something?" Marshall nodded his head toward Stiller.

"You'd better go home, Kevie-Wevie," Stiller hissed, his lips barely moving. "Mommy's expecting you."

I got in the Honda and slammed the door. How could the day get any worse? First the disagreement with Dani, then Stiller ruins my shirt, and now dopey Marshall has to show up. And when I thought about how Marshall had blown my opportunity to teach Stiller a lesson, it made me even madder.

Marshall went on and on about how he had volunteered to pick up some stuff at the store for Mom because she was so busy. And since he would be coming this way, he reasoned, it made perfect sense for him to pick me up from school. Now wasn't I glad he was so considerate of my mother?

Blah, blah, blah. Marshall tried his best to make conversation, but for me, the drive across town was as unbearable as getting a cavity filled. I didn't feel like being his little buddy. I didn't feel like helping him track down the best price on laundry detergent, either, so I waited in the car while he went in the Piggly-Wiggly. When he came back out, he had three bags of groceries and a bucket of Mom's regular detergent—plus two bottles of root beer.

On the way home, Marshall drove with one hand and held his root beer bottle in the other. He spoke between sips. "Marcy says you're working out almost every day."

I took a drink and tried to think of ways to get him to shut up. "I'm up to ten chin-ups and we're working on push-ups."

"You keep working out and you could really do damage to someone's face. I have a feeling that's what was going to happen back there."

"I can take care of him."

"That's not a good solution to your problem," Marshall said. "I've been there, and fighting only makes things worse."

I rolled my eyes and slouched in my seat. It couldn't get any worse than this.

I was wrong. I put my hand in my right pocket, and a shock zapped up my arm as if I'd jammed it into a light socket. The bait wasn't there!

For the first time since Cletus McCulley's funeral, I'd left home without the purple fishing worm in my pocket.

I helped Marshall carry the groceries upstairs and then ran straight to my room to look for the worm. I tore through the drawers, the bedcovers, and the trash can. I searched the bathroom, from behind the toilet to the medicine cabinet. Still no worm. I sat down and tried to remember the last time I had it. Then a sick feeling came over me. Mom was washing clothes when I left for school. What if I'd left it in the pocket of yesterday's jeans?

I dove into the basket of dirty laundry. The jeans weren't there. I looked through the basket of clean laundry and the clean clothes hanging on the rod beside the dryer. The jeans weren't there, either. Then I opened the dryer and found a load of clothes inside that had been dried but not folded. I dumped them onto the floor and dug through the pile until I found the jeans. When I stuck my hand in the right pocket I found the worm. It hadn't melted. It wasn't as slick and shiny as it used to be, but it was still in one piece.

Marshall put the new bucket of detergent on the shelf. "Looking for something?"

"I found it."

He pointed at the clean clothes I'd scattered on the floor. "You may want to pick those up before Mrs. K gets back. She and Mr. K went after a body, and she may not appreciate all this extra work you've made for her." Proud to be my mother's little helper, he grabbed a handful of hangers and handed me half. "We'll finish this up real quick, and then I'll go downstairs and help you get the chapel and front hall cleaned up."

Marcy had gone back to school for a few days to take some exams, and wouldn't be home until the weekend. I had no idea why Marshall was hanging around. Maybe he thought impressing us was a good way to get to Marcy. Or maybe he just liked hanging around funeral homes.

He sure wasn't doing it for the money. My parents had tried to pay him several times, but he always refused, saying he considered us friends and that we'd do the same for him. Besides, he said, he made good money at his job with an accounting firm in Gleason. If I had a good job like that, I sure wouldn't be spending my free time at the Paramount. Then again, maybe I would—if it meant I'd get to see Dani. I made a mental note to call her later and try to patch things up.

I grabbed some shirts and started putting them on the hangers. Something about the laundry smelled different. Or was it something in the room? Mom must have bought some new kind of dryer sheets, although I'd never heard of dryer sheets that smelled like aftershave. I sniffed a shirt, but the smell wasn't there. Maybe Marshall had gone a little heavy on the Old Spice. But that wasn't right, either. Only old men wore Old Spice. And Marshall didn't wear aftershave. Besides, why would he want to smell good when Marcy wasn't around?

When Marshall bent over to pick up the rest of the clothes, the hem of his shirt came untucked, revealing the waistband of his smiley-face boxers. Mom had lectured me before about making fun of Marshall, but sometimes it was hard not to, especially at a time like this. It seemed so odd that a girl as put together as Marcy would be interested in a guy as dumpy as Marshall. When he stretched his arm to reach for a stray sock, his shirt pulled up even more, exposing a long, swollen scar on his back.

"Ewww, Marshall," I said, making a face. "What happened to your back? Did you have surgery?"

Marshall jerked up and tucked in his shirt. "It's nothing. Just a scar. Forget it."

"But how did you get it? Did you donate a kidney or something?"

Marshall glared at me. "Shut up."

I'd never seen him get touchy before. He started to sweat as he reached back to make sure his shirt was still tucked in.

"Hey, I was just asking. I didn't mean to make you upset."

"Then leave me alone," Marshall said. He walked back to the kitchen. I took the worm out of my pocket and stretched it until it was more than double its original length. I hadn't really meant to upset Marshall. Even if he wasn't my favorite person, I at least admired his determination to pursue Marcy.

I heard the hearse pull into the garage. Then the word: *Apologize.* Apologize? Apologize for what?

Apologize, Kevin.

Suddenly, I knew the Old Spice smell in the laundry room wasn't from the dryer sheets. It wasn't coming from Marshall, either. The only men I knew who wore Old Spice were retired—or dead. Goose bumps popped up on my arms, and a wave of cold shot through my body so hard it made me tremble. My eyes told me I was the only person in that room, but other senses told me that I was not alone. I had the strongest feeling that Cletus McCulley was standing beside me, and it scared the crap out of me. I had to get out.

I stepped into the kitchen, keeping my neck stiff to resist the temptation to look back. Marshall was putting away the canned vegetables. "Help me get these in the cabinet before Mrs. K comes up. Kevin, what's wrong?"

"What?"

"Your face is so pale. You look like you've seen a ghost. Are you sick?"

"No," I said. "No. Listen, Marshall. I'm sorry. I didn't know asking about your scar would upset you. I won't do it again."

Marshall looked relieved. "Thanks."

I helped Marshall put the last of the groceries away. Mom came in, and Marshall gave her back the change from the grocery money. She gave him a hug in return. "Marshall, you're such a fine young man. Arlice and I appreciate your help so much."

"No problem, Mrs. K."

"And believe it or not, it means more to Marcy than you think."

Marshall's face lit up. "You really think so?"

"I know so. She told me herself."

I slipped past them and started down the stairs. I would have liked to know exactly what Marcy had said to Mom about Marshall, but the afternoon was almost gone, and Dad was expecting me to vacuum the front hall and the chapel.

I was getting the Super Vac out of the big maintenance closet at the bottom of the stairs when Marshall came up behind me and grabbed my arm. "Listen, Kevin. I'm not proud of the things I did when I was younger. I can't go back and change any of it. Don't make the same mistakes I did. Don't ever do anything out of pride that you'll wish you could take back someday. You were almost right about my kidney. I didn't donate it. I lost it. In a fight. I was stabbed. I almost died."

Our goofy, blubbery Marshall fighting like

a tough guy? It was hard to imagine, but the tremor in his voice and the sweat beading on his upper lip told me he wasn't kidding. "How did you end up fighting someone with a knife? Were you in a gang or something?

"Let's just say I was trying to be part of a group where I didn't belong."

"But Marshall—"

"Do me a favor." He lowered his voice and looked over both shoulders before locking eyes with me. "Don't talk to Marcy about it. And don't ask me about it again."

His grip on my arm tightened. "OK," I said. "I won't tell."

Marshall left me alone in the closet and entered the chapel just as Mom finished descending the stairs. I walked out of the closet and she gave me a hug. "How was school today?"

"Fine," I said. "No problems."

She laughed and nodded her head toward the chapel. "You know, Kev, if Marshall keeps pursuing Marcy, our funeral home may get to host a wedding!"

Chapter Fifteen

Marcy came home from school early Friday morning, the day before Valentine's Day. I ran up the steps of her apartment and gave her a hug.

"Hey Kev!" Marcy hugged me back. "How's Mr. and Mrs. K?"

"Everything's OK, but it's sure been quiet here without you. You wanna play cards tonight?"

"I may not be able to. It depends on if I hear from Marshall today and if he has any plans. But I'm sure I can find time this weekend to beat you at a game. Did you do your workouts while I was gone?"

I stood up a little straighter. "Of course," I said, and flexed my biceps. "I've got to keep up my manly physique."

Marcy gave me a playful shove. "Get out of here, squirt, or you're gonna be late for school."

This was going to be a great day, I could tell. It started with my first entry in Volume VI, where, thanks to a fresh inch of snow, I'd recorded my best animal sightings for the year so far—two robins, a red cardinal, one raccoon, and a set of deer tracks that led back to the woods. We had a funeral that afternoon, but none scheduled for the next day. Marcy was home, and in just an hour or so I'd see Dani. And tomorrow would be Valentine's Day.

At school, I received the ultimate stroke of good luck—Stiller was absent. Dani was still mad about our little misunderstanding, so she was cold during first hour. But I was confident I could soften her up.

At lunch, I slid into our booth as usual. "Hey Dani. What's up?"

She chewed her fish stick and didn't answer. I took a sandwich and bottle of juice out of my sack and placed them in front of me. Then I unwrapped my apple and set the bigger half on her plate. She picked it up and examined it, then shrugged and set it back down.

I ignored her casual attitude toward my gift of goodwill. "Got any plans for lunch tomorrow?"

She still didn't answer, but I saw the pink begin to creep up her cheeks, and I knew I had her. I pressed on. "Dad's taking Mom to the Cow Palace tomorrow and he asked me if I wanted to go and invite someone. So I'm inviting you. How about it?"

Her long brown hair, which she'd tossed over her shoulders, fell down again, covering the sides of her face. She peeked at me from under her bangs and I saw just a glimmer of metal between her lips. "Sure. How about if my mom just drops me off at the home?"

"Great. Come over about noon." I smiled at her and she smiled back, this time with a real Dani smile. We didn't talk anymore during lunch, but I walked with her to our next class, and when I left her at her desk, she gave my arm a little squeeze. My feet didn't touch the floor the rest of the day.

Marcy picked me up after school. As soon as I got in her VW, I knew she was going out with Marshall. She always looked immaculate, even in sweats. But today she was especially pretty in a foamy green cashmere sweater and black leather slacks. Someone like her should have been riding in a limo, not shifting gears in a rusty old Beetle. I asked where she was going.

Marcy tried to give me the evil eye but giggled when I batted my eyelashes at her. "I was gonna say it's none of your business, but since you'll bug me 'til I answer, I'll tell you. We're going to Memphis to meet Marshall's mother and grandmother, and then tonight he's got tickets to take us all to the Memphis Orchestra. Afterward we'll spend the night at his mother's house, and we'll drive back to Armadillo tomorrow. What big plans do you have for your sweetie?"

My face burned. "She's not my sweetie. She's just a good friend. Actually, she's the only friend I have."

The traffic signal ahead of us turned yellow. Marcy slowed to a stop. "Hey," Marcy said, "I'm your friend too."

"You can't be my friend. You're my sister."

Marcy looked at me. I smiled. I couldn't believe what I'd just said, but I'd been feeling it, and I guess it was time for it to come out. I'd said it like it was the most natural thing in the world—but it had to be, because I felt so good inside now that I'd said it. I did feel like Marcy was my sister. It made Marcy feel good too, I could tell. At first she didn't answer. Then her eyes went soft, and she smiled back with a sweet, loving kind of smile. Then she whacked me in the back of the head.

"That's the way it goes with the chicks, little brother. I may need to keep an eye on this Dani person. 'Cuz first, you're friends, then before you know it—chomp! The love bug takes a big bite out of you. Just watch it in case she tries to spit you back out!"

Marshall drove Marcy to Memphis in Dad's S-10. So the next day Dani and I sat in the back seat of Marshall's red Honda and Dad took us all to the Cow Palace for lunch. We sat in Mom's favorite booth—the one overlooking the pasture—and Dad ordered the Sweethearts Special: a giant chopped steak in the shape of a heart served on a large platter with two baked potatoes, two Caesar salads, and two cloverleaf rolls. I had my usual quarter-pound Cow Pattie with fries. Dani got the special Love Me Chicken Tenders basket that came with a bowl of heart-shaped gelatin salad. As we waited for our orders, Dad slipped a brightly wrapped box out from under his coat and handed it to Mom.

"This is for my best friend," he said. He rubbed the dimple in Mom's chin with his index finger and kissed the tip of her nose.

"Oh Arlice," she said, smoothing an invisible wisp of thinning hair behind his ear, "you're so swell."

Swell? Only my mother would say something totally stupid like that. I ducked my head to hide my smirk. Dani's head was ducked too, her hand over her mouth, stifling her giggles. She looked so cute. My parents had no idea we were laughing at them.

Mom ripped the paper, and her lips formed into a large O. "Oh Arlice, how did you know?"

Mom and Dad were too caught up in the moment to hear me snort, but Dani sure heard me because she kicked me in the leg really hard to make me shut up. But I couldn't help it. Who else but my mom would get excited about *The Three Stooges Video Collection?* You'd think Dad had given her tickets for a Caribbean cruise. She hopped up and down in the booth and flung her arms around Dad's neck. "You are so sweet! You always buy me the best presents!"

The waitress brought our plates, interrupting the lovefest. I was glad Dani and I ordered our own meals. The Sweetheart Special, as I said, came on one big platter—which meant my lovebird parents were supposed to share. Although I liked Dani, I still preferred to keep our germs separate.

I had a gift for Dani, but I wanted to wait for the right moment to give it to her. After lunch we went back to the home and played two killer games of Monopoly. Mom and Dad played the first game with us. Dani and I played the second one alone. She beat me both times.

At dusk we sat out in the back lot together so she could help me put that night's entry in

Volume VI. We hadn't been outside long before the clouds began to thicken, which helped the darkness to fall faster than usual. I figured I'd better not wait much longer. I pulled the flat package out of my coat.

"Dani, this is for you," I said, and handed it to her.

I got the reaction I'd hoped for—another big smile. Dani tore the paper carefully.

"Oh Kevin." She brushed her mittened hand across the soft leather journal cover. "It's beautiful."

"Open it."

She read aloud the short message I'd written inside:

> TO DANI–
>
> Thank you for being my best friend.
>
> Kevin

She gave me a quick, awkward hug. One of her tears, cooled by the February air, lingered on my cheek.

"I want to tell you something," Dani said. "But I don't want you to be mad at me."

"Sure." What I really wanted to say was, "How could I ever be mad at a girl as beautiful as you?"

"Well, you know Daddy's the branch president at our church, and it's hard sometimes not to overhear things—"

I could hear her speak, but I was paying more attention to the pupils of her eyes as they widened in the dim light.

"I don't want you to think I'm being your friend just because I'm trying to get you to come to church, or to help your parents come back to church."

"You know about my parents being Mormons?"

Dani nodded. "The correct name is Latter-day Saints. And yes, I overheard Mom and Dad talking one night—something about your parents losing a baby right after they were baptized. Your mom told my dad about it. Oh Kevin, it sounds so sad. But then I started thinking, what if Kevin thinks I'm only being nice to him because I want him to come to church? I would want to be your friend, no matter what."

Dani's confession was so sincere, and the look on her face so earnest, that I was glad she knew about my family. I put my gloved hand over her mittened one and squeezed it tight.

We sat for a long time without speaking, then she said, "Kevin, promise me something."

"What?" I would have bungee jumped off the Mississippi River Bridge if she'd asked me to.

She gazed out beyond the trees, to where the purple sky deepened into black. "There's no good reason for you to fight Chuck. The only reason you want to is pride. You don't want people to think you're afraid of him. But that's no reason. I'm not saying don't defend yourself if he hits you, but fighting because he embarrasses you isn't right. You don't have to prove anything to anyone, especially me."

Then our eyes met, and for a split second the clouds parted just enough for the moon to shine through. The light transformed Dani's perfect brown irises into pure gold. "Please promise me."

I sat there, stunned and speechless, and let her voice wash over me. "Promise me, Kevin, you won't fight Chuck Stiller unless he's trying to hurt you."

A slight gust of wind nudged the clouds back over the moon, but now Dani shimmered as if she had swallowed it whole. At that moment, I knew there wasn't anyone or anything more beautiful than Danielle Angeline Carter. A spark ignited in my chest that blazed into a fireball. It was cold enough outside to see your breath, but I was sweating so bad that I knew steam had to be coming off my forehead. I'd seen TV documentaries about spontaneous human combustion, and now I believed it was true. I knew any second I'd burst into flames from the neck down, leaving nothing behind but my arms, legs, a charred coat, and my head with a dumb expression on my face.

And I wanted to kiss her. More than anything, I wanted to kiss her. I wanted to tell her that I loved her. I wanted to lean over and kiss Danielle Angeline Carter right in the center of her soft pink lips.

But I didn't. I just sat there, my mind numb from the rush of emotion. "OK. Whatever you want."

"Kevin, listen to me." Dani shook my arm, trying to get my attention. "I mean it, Kevin. I don't want you to get hurt."

Her words snapped me out of the love-spell. She thought I'd get hurt? Was she saying I couldn't take care of myself? "What do you mean, get hurt? Do you think I'm a wimp or something?"

Dani crossed her arms and turned away. "See, that's just what I'm talking about. You're worried about what others think, not if you're doing the right thing." She stood up, and I realized the temperature outside was still thirty-two degrees. "Just remember, Kevin, that what matters is how you feel about what you've done, not how other people feel about it. If you look back and wish you'd done something different, there won't be any good excuse for you. You'll never be able to change the fact that you caved in to Stiller instead of standing on higher ground." She got up and headed back to the home.

I jumped up and ran after her. I knew she was right. I had no doubt. I'd known all along that fighting Stiller wouldn't solve anything. It would only give me something to brag about. I'd be hurting him for my own gain, as a warning to others that I couldn't be pushed around.

I thought about the worm in my pocket. I hadn't been able to put it into words before, and now Dani had done it for me without even knowing it. If I looked back and wished I'd done something different, I wouldn't have a good excuse. That's why Mom talked Dad into buying the Paramount. Why Cletus McCulley stuck with his buddies in the war, and by his wife when she was sick. And why Marshall would give anything to go back and change what he'd done as a teenager. I reached in my pocket. The worm was still there. I caught up to Dani as she entered the garden outside the guest kitchen. I grabbed her shoulders and spun her around.

"Dani, I promise you I won't fight Chuck Stiller." I looked at her with more sincerity than I'd ever looked at anyone. "And I mean it."

My chest began to burn again. My face moved in slow motion, closer and closer to hers. My hands slipped around her waist, and her arms floated onto my shoulders. Just as I started to close my eyes, Dani's words echoed again in my mind: *If you look back and wish you'd done something different, you won't have a good excuse.* And for reasons I still don't understand, at the last second I turned my face so that my lips, instead of meeting hers, brushed against her soft cheek.

Dani giggled, sounding oddly like my mother. "Oh Kevin," she said, drawing me close for a hug. "You're the best!"

Suddenly, there was a loud crash in the guest kitchen. Dani and I squatted behind the holly bushes and sneaked a look through the French doors. Marcy and Marshall were having an argument. They wandered around the room. Marcy was in the lead, flailing her arms and yelling at the top of her lungs while Marshall tagged behind. He wiped his forehead with his right hand as he used his other hand to place what looked like a small jewelry box on the table.

We slipped around to the front entrance, down the hall, and stood to the side of the slightly open kitchen door. We couldn't figure out what they were fighting about, but they sure were mad.

"We never agree on this, Marshall," Marcy yelled, "never, ever!"

"Who says we have to agree?" Marshall yelled back. "Just because you say so doesn't make it right! Can't we politely agree to disagree?"

Dani looked at me and shrugged her shoulders. This made no sense at all.

Marcy moved to the center of the kitchen and began pacing back and forth, her hands on her hips. "I don't understand you, Marshall Cartwright. I just don't understand you."

"I thought I understood you, but I guess I was wrong. Maybe all this time I've been wrong about us, too." Marshall put on his coat. "I love you, Marcy, more that anyone I've ever known. I thought that, I mean I hoped that, you would learn to feel the same way about me. But maybe I've been wrong about that, too."

He stepped toward the French doors leading out to the garden, and turned to her as if it were the last time he'd ever see her again.

"I'm so sorry, Marcy. Sorry for everything. I'll always love you, but if I make you this miserable, I won't stay around any longer."

He left. The lock clicked shut. Marcy's bottom lip quivered.

"Ohmigosh," Dani whispered. "I think Marshall just proposed to Marcy."

Marcy stroked her finger across the top of the black velvet box on the table. Then she picked it up and opened it.

"Oh Kevin, it's an engagement ring!" Dani squeaked, her hands over her heart. "He must have spent a fortune on it. I can see the diamond from here."

Then Marcy started bawling. She stomped her feet. Was she throwing a tantrum? Although I'd never been all that nice to Marshall, I did feel sorrier for him at that moment than I did Marcy. After all, it took a lot of nerve on his part to ask someone as pigheaded as Marcy to be his wife.

Then all at once Marcy stopped crying. Her body snapped to attention. Her eyes grew round and wide, and she clapped her hands over her mouth like she was trying to keep from losing her last breath. She charged toward the door and raced out, passing Dani and me without even seeing us. We followed her out the front entrance. She ran in her bare feet down the slushy sidewalk to the side parking lot. Marshall was just a few steps away from his car.

"Marshall, wait!" Marcy screamed. "Don't go!"

She pounced on Marshall and, grabbing his face in her hands, kissed him on his chin, cheeks, and forehead. It was hard to tell whether she was laughing or crying. "Don't go, Marshall. I love you. I know I do. I've just been too scared to admit it. Oh Marshall, I do love you." She dropped down on one knee and held his hand against her tear-covered cheek. "Marshall Cartwright, please marry me. Will you? Will you marry me?"

Marshall wiped his eyes with his free hand. "You always think you have to have the last word," he said. "But guess what? This time I get to say it. Yes. Yes, Marcy, more than anything in the world, I want to marry you."

Marcy stood up, and Marshall held her close. As he kissed her—one of those long, passionate, soap opera kisses—the tiniest, most delicate flakes of snow began to fall. And Marshall lifted Marcy up so her bare feet wouldn't have to touch the cold, damp ground.

Chapter Sixteen

Marcy picked April 4 as her wedding day, mainly because she wanted to get it over with before her final exams in May. But she also wanted to get married in Mom's garden when the spring flowers were in bloom.

So Mom was right—it looked like we were going to host a wedding. A year ago, I would have thought that was the dumbest thing I'd ever heard of. But now it not only seemed right, it felt as normal as if we were hosting it in the backyard of our old house. Had my idea of normal changed that much in just a year? Maybe it wasn't the idea of normal that was different now, but the idea of what I believed home to be.

The weeks leading up to the big day were hectic. Every day we had either a visitation or a funeral. At school, the seventh-grade class had standardized testing, so we spent two full weeks filling in the bubbles on computer answer sheets with our #2 pencils. Plus we had field trips and end-of-term projects. The only reason I survived at all was because I had the wedding and spring break to look forward to.

Though I was busy, my life was better than ever. There were two reasons for that. One was Dani. After Valentine's Day, my feelings for her changed a lot. We'd developed a deeper kind of friendship, even though we never got mushy about it. I didn't try to kiss her again, and I think she appreciated that. I'd always thought girls wanted to be kissed, but I don't think Dani did. I knew she liked me, but I think she felt like I respected her feelings, which meant more to her than if I'd told her she was pretty all the time. Dani was a no-nonsense, cerebral kind of girl. She wasn't an airhead or flirty. Our personalities were perfectly matched.

Second, Stiller was less of a nuisance. I was determined to keep my promise to Dani, and so whenever Stiller started up his old tricks, I ignored him. If he tried to annoy me, I walked away. A few times I even tried being pleasant, smiling and saying hi if I saw him in the hall. But I don't think it was my change in attitude that affected him. I began to think more about what Dani said, that maybe Chuck Stiller did have problems.

Stiller had never looked clean to me. Of course I was kind of a neat freak, but I wondered if I judged him too harshly. Sometimes he looked like he just needed to wash up. But lately bathing and washing his hair hadn't ranked very high on his list of priorities. Some days he wore the same clothes to school three days in a row. And that was on the days he showed up. By the time spring break rolled around, Stiller had missed more classes than he'd attended. It didn't hurt my feelings, but I never said anything to Dani. It made my promise to her easier to keep.

Three days before the wedding, Mom and Dad brought in the body of the Armadillo postmaster. Irene Goodacre, a widow who lived on Fiddle Creek Road just off Highway 9, went to get her mail that afternoon and saw the mail truck sitting outside. She found the postmaster dead in the front seat, his arm stuck out the window and inside her mailbox, still clutching her mail—which included her monthly Social Security check. When my parents arrived, the old woman was throwing a fit because she'd had to wait so long for someone to get the check out of his hand that the bank had already closed.

Everyone in Armadillo knew the postmaster, so we were busy during those three days. That, plus preparations for Marcy's wedding, was enough to make Mom need medication.

There were only going to be seven people at the wedding—the bride and groom, our family, and Marshall's mother and grandmother. In the beginning, Marcy made Mom promise that she wouldn't go to a lot of trouble. So Mom told Marcy not to worry, she would order a small cake from Wal-Mart and be done with it. She ordered the cake, and also bought two cans of party peanuts, a box of pastel mints, plus two liters of lemon-lime soda and a half gallon of orange sherbet to make punch. Mom seemed satisfied with that. Then the day before the wedding, she insisted she had time to fix all those dainty reception foods, like cucumber sandwiches and ham rolls on toothpicks.

I thought Dad had a great suggestion. "Let's have some barbecue brought in and be done with it," he said. "Everyone stays for supper, and we'll all have a great time."

Mom said if Dad didn't have any more class than that then we might as well feed everybody TV dinners. Dad replied that TV dinners would taste better than eating white bread with cream cheese on it.

Mom's right eyebrow raised until it looked like an inverted V. "Are you saying I can't cook?"

Dad tried to dig himself out of the hole, but without meaning to, he dug it deeper. "Well, Freda, even if you had the time to fix all this food, you're not quite ready for the Pillsbury Bake-Off."

He was trying to make things easier, but he might as well have told Mom she could ruin a recipe for pig slop because that was the way she took it. She locked herself in the bedroom.

Dad shook his head. "Your mother tries to do too much sometimes," he said. Then he gave me a lopsided grin. "It's just because she has a big heart. That's why I married her." He then called the manager of the Cow Palace and reserved the private dining area so we could all go there for a reception dinner. The manager even agreed to let us bring our own cake.

On the morning of Marcy's wedding the National Weather Service issued a severe thunderstorm watch for Sherman and all surrounding counties until 6 P.M. I didn't take it too seriously since the sky was clear, but Dad said he was glad the postmaster's funeral was going to be early. We'd be through by noon, in plenty of time to help Mom with Marcy's wedding at four. Maybe by then the storms would move to the northeast.

During the postmaster's funeral service I set up chairs for the wedding in the sitting area. All the bulbs we'd planted in the fall were blooming—huge bunches of daffodils and tulips lined the walks and bordered the wall. The last of the crocuses popped through the mulch like multi-colored popcorn, and the hyacinths stood proud with buds erupting in bright Easter colors.

I set up the chairs and tied on the white bows Mom had fixed the night before. The garden was so full of life; you'd never imagine you were standing just outside the doors of a funeral home.

I remembered what Dad said the day we ate our first lunch at the Cow Palace: Death is a part of life. But just one part, I thought. Love is a part of life. So are friendships, weddings, and babies. Change is a part of life too. Even unpleasant changes like moving, or losing your old job and starting a new one. Even sad changes, like death. There were so many parts of life I'd never given any thought to before, not until we moved to the Paramount.

Marshall's mother and grandmother arrived after lunch. Mrs. Cartwright was friendly enough. But Granny Allen, who looked to be a couple of years shy of a century, was superstitious and scared out of her mind. She walked around clutching her cane to her chest as if it were her only defense against evil spirits.

"It's bad luck for them to marry here," she said. "I'm tellin' you, these young 'uns are temptin' the Devil himself if they say their vows in this place."

The first clouds appeared around 3:00 P.M. I checked the local forecast, and the radar showed a line of thunderstorms headed for Sherman County and Armadillo. Mom was braiding Marcy's hair. She started to cry.

Marcy patted her hand. "Don't cry, Mrs. K. Nothin's gonna ruin my wedding. God can send a tornado if he wants, but I'm having my wedding outside."

By 3:30, the temperature had dropped ten degrees. A blanket of black clouds threatened overhead. Marshall begged and Granny Allen wailed about curses being brought upon our heads, but Marcy refused to move the ceremony indoors. So Dad and Marshall got out one of the tarps we used for graveside services and set it up in the garden. It was navy blue with white trim and the name PARAMOUNT screen printed in white on both sides. President Carter had agreed to perform the ceremony, and he arrived just as Dad hammered the last stake into the ground.

At six minutes till four we gathered under the tent—everyone, that is, except Granny Allen. It was bad enough to get married at a funeral home, she said, but if you're going to stand under the graveside tent to do it, then you just might as well ask Lucifer to let you have it, and she wasn't going to be party to the ruination of her grandson's marriage. She dug in her orthopedic heels and there was nothing Marshall or his frustrated mother could say to make Granny budge from the kitchen doorway.

Mrs. Cartwright said, "Mama, you can stand there rooted like an old mule if you want, but I'm gonna see my baby get married. And it don't matter if he's getting married in a funeral home, a nursing home, or the county jail. Just stand there and be stubborn. I don't care. Come on, Marshall." She grabbed his arm and yanked him out the door. Granny Allen shook her head, rolled her eyes up to heaven, and muttered prayers under her breath.

The timer on my watch signaled four—my cue to turn on the CD player. Mom stepped around Granny Allen and took her place in front as the matron of honor. I heard the plop of a large raindrop as it hit the tarp.

Dad reached inside the door and guided Marcy out. The guy who said angels had to have wings would have changed his mind if he'd seen Marcy float out in the cloud of white lace that was her wedding dress. She slipped her arm through Dad's and kissed him on the cheek. He covered her hand with his, and they started down the aisle. Granny Allen pleaded with God to spare us of His wrath. Marshall kept his eyes on Marcy, and a single tear ran down the side of his nose. Sweat beaded his forehead, and he looked as if any minute he would melt into a big blob with a tuxedo on top.

President Carter spoke solemnly. "Who gives this bride away?"

Dad turned to Marcy. "Her mother and I do." They hugged, and Dad shifted over to stand beside Marshall as his best man. Marcy hugged Mom too, and gave her the bouquet of Easter lilies to hold. The raindrops began to hit louder and faster. Marshall took Marcy's hand. A sudden gust of wind blew two of the white bows off the chairs.

Mother Nature decided to illuminate the vows with some of her own fireworks. A bright flash electrified the sky. President Carter said, "If there be anyone who believes this couple should not marry, speak now or forever hold your peace." Ground-cracking thunder followed.

"Oh, Lordy Lordy Lordy," wailed Granny Allen. "The Lord is wreaking out His vengeance on us today!"

Marshall moved closer to Marcy. Mom's eyes bulged out and her neck turned red. Dad leaned out from under the tarp to look at the sky and got hit between the eyes by a big raindrop. He shook his head and wiped the water from his face with a handkerchief.

Just as the happy couple finished repeating their vows, something hit the back of my neck—a stone of pea-sized hail. By the time Marcy said the I do part, the hail had grown to the size of ping-pong balls.

Dad had been in such a hurry to get the tarp up earlier that he didn't do a great job of securing it. The tarp started to droop under the weight of the rain and ice, and the poles leaned with the wind. Another bright flash and window-rattling boom, and President Carter shouted, "I now pronounce you husband and wife, and I suggest we go inside!"

I grabbed the CD player, and Granny Allen prayed over each one of us as we ran into the guest kitchen. Dad was the last one in. He shut the door and turned just in time to see the tarp blow over. The power went out, and the emergency lights came on.

Marcy grabbed Marshall's arm and dragged him to the center of the room. "President, you forgot the most important part of the ceremony. You've got to tell Mr. Cartwright to kiss his bride! Kevin, turn that music back on!"

I punched in track five and started the recessional. President Carter tidied his jacket, and then spread his arms out toward the couple. "Ladies and gentlemen, I present to you Mr. and Mrs. Marshall Cartwright. You, sir, may kiss this bride."

Marshall lifted the veil, uncovering Marcy's perfect teeth and almond eyes. They kissed. Marshall's mother cried. Granny Allen praised the Lord and said we'd been spared eternal damnation. Dad stood behind Mom, his arms around her waist. Maybe it was because his clothes were soaking wet, but he looked taller. And there was a softness to his face I'd never seen before—a gentle glow that flowed over his skin like the afternoon rain. And then I heard the voice: *Kelsey is here.*

I took the worm out of my right pocket. My parents had cared for Marcy these past few months, and she had cared about us. She was part of our family. Maybe I was hearing the voice wrong.

Kelsey is here, and your father knows it.

In my heart, I wished I could see her, if only for a second.

And there she was, my sister Kelsey, dressed in white, all grown up with long black hair and Mom's eyes. She stood beside my father, gazing up at him, the same sweet expression of love—and contentment—on her face. But I'd only wished for a second. One blink, and she was gone.

Then I knew. I knew why Kelsey was there. Dad had accepted her death. Maybe it had something to do with the way my parents felt about Marcy. Maybe caring about Marcy as if she was a daughter made him realize that he still had those feelings for Kelsey, even though she was dead. And having those feelings was OK.

For the first time, the Paramount felt like home. I felt so much love then for my parents, for Kelsey, for Marcy—heck, even lumpy, dumpy Marshall had a few redeeming qualities. I wished the happiness and closeness to my family I felt in that kitchen, even in the whole funeral home that I once thought would be such a gruesome place, would last forever. And at that moment I knew, without any doubt, that just as we'd taken care of Marcy, Kelsey was being taken care of too.

My dead friend Cletus McCulley would see to that.

Chapter Seventeen

While the newlyweds were on their honeymoon, we had another one of our kitchen-table board meetings.

"Arlice, we've already talked about offering Marcy a permanent job," Mom said. "I think we should consider hiring Marshall, too."

"Why? He's got a good job in Gleason."

"We need him, Arlice," Mom said. She sighed and drew imaginary squiggles on the table with her finger. "This business is too big for the three of us."

I spoke up. "I think it's a good idea. He could keep the books and continue doing odd jobs for us."

"If we don't offer them something here, then someone else will. Marcy's been too much help to me for us to let her go. And you have to admit that Marshall's been handy to have around."

Dad nodded. "Without him, we couldn't have finished those remodeling projects on time."

Mom went to the fridge for a ginger ale. "Kevin's busy with school, and he'll have more activities. You and I need some time to ourselves so we can get away and not live the business twenty-four-seven. If all Marshall does is handle the bookkeeping, that will take a huge load off our shoulders. It's a full-time job now to keep the records and pay bills. And I think we've established ourselves enough to afford two full-time employees."

That's what Mom said. But I could read her eyes, and they said something else: *I couldn't bear to see Marcy go. Please, let's give her a job so she'll stay, and Marshall too.*

I could read Dad's eyes too. He understood.

"I make a motion that we hire Mr. and Mrs. Marshall Cartwright," I said, raising my arm. "Anyone second?"

"Me," Mom said.

Dad slapped the table. "The motion's been made and seconded. All in favor?"

"Aye."

"That does it. The vote is unanimous. We'll present them an offer when they come back."

Two weeks later Marcy and Marshall returned from their honeymoon—a fifty-mile canoe trip on the Current River near Eminence, Missouri. Marcy glowed, but Marshall was wiped out. The most primitive place he'd ever slept was a Motel 6, which was still better than sleeping in a tent on a riverbank. And he was no Boy Scout. He'd tried to impress Marcy by climbing a tree, but it happened to be a tree covered in poison oak. When they came home, Marshall was covered in itchy, red blisters. For several days, he had to stay in their apartment because he couldn't stand anything touching his skin but calamine lotion.

Even in his miserable state, Marshall was thrilled when Dad phoned him with our job offer. He said that he and Marcy had even talked during the trip about how nice it would be if both of them could work for us. So when Marcy left for her finals, it was official—she and Marshall were full-time employees of the Paramount.

We drove back to our old hometown for Marcy's graduation. We left early in the morning so we could see our old neighborhood. The factory where Dad had once worked was still vacant. We passed my old school and drove down our old street. We even stopped and talked to the couple living in our old house. I got to see my old room, now a nursery for twin baby boys. The Hot Wheels wallpaper that Mom had put up when I was in kindergarten was still there. My old swing set was still in the backyard, too. But everything looked so much smaller than I'd remembered.

The speeches at Marcy's graduation were boring, but it was fun to see her walk across the stage and get her diploma. She drove back home that night to be with Marshall, but we stayed at the Owl's Nest Bed and Breakfast until Sunday morning.

As we were driving home Sunday, Marcy called on our cell phone. There had been a call to pick up the body of a nineteen-year-old boy. He'd been drinking, and when a state trooper tried to pull him over, he sped off, forcing the trooper into a high-speed chase. The boy lost control and crashed into an eighteen-wheeler. On Monday morning, the *Armadillo Courier's* headline read, DRUNK TEEN DIES IN FATAL CRASH.

There was a photo of the big truck with a tangled heap of metal piled in front. If that had been a car once, you couldn't tell. I shuddered, thinking about what that boy must have looked like when they found him. I read the report under the photo:

> The Arkansas State Police and the Sherman County Sheriff's office were called to the scene of a tragic accident just past the Armadillo exit on Interstate 55. Last night at 2:14 A.M., Derek Lee Stiller was killed after trying to elude police during a high-speed chase north on the interstate. He lost control of his Camaro and skidded into the southbound lane, colliding head-on with a semi driven by Thomas Howton of Pocahontas, Arkansas, who was not injured. Stiller was killed instantly. Tests by the Armadillo Community Hospital and the State Police determined that Stiller's blood alcohol level was three times the legal limit. Funeral arrangements are pending at Paramount Funeral Home in Armadillo. SEE PAGE A3 FOR COMPLETE OBITUARY.

I didn't realize he was related to Chuck Stiller until I turned the page and saw his picture. He had the same smirk, the same sandy blond hair, and the same close-set eyes as the Stiller who'd tormented me for so many months.

I read the obituary carefully. Derek Lee Stiller was survived by his father, Stan, and his brother, Charles. So this guy was Stiller's older brother. He was preceded in death by his mother, Anna Leigh Stiller. There was no mention of a stepmother or grandparents. There were uncles, but all from out of state.

Stiller's mother had been dead for over ten years. When she died, Chuck was just a baby. Chuck Stiller had never even known his mother.

I was reading the obituary in the guest kitchen when Marcy came in for some bottled water. She sat down beside me and motioned to the paper. "It was a pretty ugly scene, Kev."

"Yeah, I'll bet."

"I remember when that boy's mother died," Marcy said. "That was pretty ugly too."

"How's that?"

"Anna Stiller's body was found in the White River. She'd been missing for several days. At first they thought she'd been murdered, then they found she'd taken a whole bottle of sleeping pills. The police ruled it a suicide, but a lot of people in town didn't believe it. Some think her husband had something to do with it, whether he drove her to do it or if he did it to her on purpose. He has a higher opinion of himself than most people have of him."

I remembered Dani's words at lunch the day of our first argument. *Maybe he has a problem.* I got a sick feeling deep in my stomach.

At school, I looked for Dani. She was finishing an essay for English. I scooted my chair close to hers. "Did you hear about Chuck's brother?"

Her eyes were sad, and my heart melted. No wonder I liked her so much. She was so compassionate. "Wasn't that terrible?"

"Marcy told me about Chuck's mother and how she died. That sure explains a lot about him."

Her response was quick and clipped. "What's that supposed to mean?"

Afraid that I hadn't said what I meant to say, I thought for a second before I answered.

"What I mean is, Stiller's had a difficult life. He never knew his mom. And with all the talk about what happened to her, he's probably confused. I feel sorry for him."

I put my hand in my pocket. The worm was there as usual. I continued. "You were right, Dani. He does have problems. I'm glad I left him alone." And when I said that, I meant it. I was glad Dani didn't back off from what she believed was right. Real friends aren't afraid to be honest, even when they're telling you something they know you don't want to hear.

I couldn't deny I'd heard the words, *Walk away* the first time Chuck wanted to fight. Cletus McCulley had something to do with that. And I was glad he didn't back off, either.

Who'd have thought a person could have friends who were living *and* dead?

The afternoon of Derek Stiller's visitation, I put on my black suit and the orange tie with the pinto bean dots. Mom asked me to help with the flowers, so I ran down to the front entrance and met the driver as she was going back to her van for more arrangements. I followed her outside. A black Corvette was sitting at the edge of the parking lot. A man inside rolled the window down and threw a bottle into the culvert on the side of the road. I grabbed two pots of ivy and headed back inside.

At the front of the chapel, a lone figure sat lifeless in the first pew, his head against the wall. It was Stiller. I walked up and set the ivy on the stands on either side of the closed casket. Derek's body was so busted up during the crash that his casket wouldn't be opened. But his senior portrait was on an easel in front of the casket. He'd been a nice-looking guy.

I sat down beside Stiller. His eyes were red and puffy. The rest of him was clean for a change. "Hey, Chuck."

He didn't answer.

"I'm sorry about your brother," I said, hoping he'd realize I was sincere. The next thing I knew, his fist cracked my jaw. The blow stunned me, knocking me off the pew and onto the floor. I stood up and rubbed my cheek.

"Get away from me, Kevin," he scowled. Snot started running from his nose, and his eyes were glassy and unresponsive. "Get away from me." He slumped his head back against the wall and rubbed his fist across his eyes. "Please, just get away from me."

I didn't want to argue with Chuck. I didn't want to hit him back. And believe it or not, I wasn't even mad that he'd hit me. I looked back at him as I left the chapel. He was cowered in the corner of the pew like an injured dog—afraid of the pain, afraid of where he was, and afraid of the circumstances that had put him there. And it was only natural for him to lash out at what he didn't understand.

Chapter Eighteen

I took my place at the front door. My jaw still throbbed from Stiller's punch. It was beginning to swell, and I hoped it didn't look too bad. Visitation was about to start, and there wasn't time to put ice on it or even splash it with cold water. So in spite of the heat I felt rising from my jawbone, I tried to pretend like nothing happened.

Of course, Mom would have to notice. She walked past me, then did a double take.

"Kevin, honey, what in the world did you do to your face?"

"It's fine, Mom."

She touched it gently, but I still flinched. "My gosh, Kevin, this looks awful!" She leaned into my face, giving me that suspicious mother expression. "I think you'd better tell me what's going on."

"Nothin' Mom. It's fine—probably just a zit."

She pointed at her face. "Do I look stupid to you?" That one was too easy. I started to make a cute remark but she put her hand over my mouth. "Never mind that," she said. "Since you don't want to talk, I won't press—but if your jaw starts bothering you, let me know, and I'll get Marcy to fill in for you." She patted my good cheek and left to check the chapel. I thought about how Stiller had never known his mother. Mom got on my nerves sometimes, but even though I'd been mad at her about the move—and about Kelsey—I hoped I'd never know what life would be like without her.

The black Corvette was still in the parking lot. A man in a dark pinstriped suit got out and walked to the door. He passed me like I was invisible. He was tall and had sandy blond hair. He wore sunglasses but didn't take them off when he came inside. And there was a sweet, yeasty smell about him, one I wasn't familiar with.

He stood in the hall with his hands in his pockets, jingling his keys. Marcy walked by, and he raised his sunglasses. He watched her as she walked to the guest kitchen. It was the only time I saw his eyes the whole night.

Mom stepped out of the chapel. "Mr. Stiller," she said as she reached out to shake his hand, "is there anything you need?"

So this was Chuck's dad. He pulled a handkerchief from his pocket and dabbed his eyes underneath his glasses. "That's kind of you Mrs. Kirk—or may I call you Freda?" He stopped wiping his tears long enough to run his index finger across her name tag. He was still holding her other hand. I began to wonder just how wet his handkerchief really was.

Mom began to fidget. "Mrs. Kirk would be better," she said as she pulled her hand away from his. "But if you need anything, let us know."

Mr. Sincerity dabbed his eyes again. "You've been so kind. I don't know how to thank you. This has been so hard for me." He put his arm around Mom's waist, and her face turned red. She peeled his arm away. I forgot about my hot jaw. Now my whole face was on fire. The jerk was flirting with my mother!

I held my radio behind my back and beeped Mom's. She looked at me and understood. "If you need something, Mr. Stiller, any member of our staff will be glad to help. Now if you'll excuse me," she said, "I have to assist my husband." Mom removed her radio from her belt and nodded at me, then went into the office. Dad was in there, filling out paperwork. Later, I saw her go upstairs. She didn't come down again the rest of the night.

The next day during lunch, I told Dani everything. "I don't know Chuck's dad," she said, "I just know what I've heard about him from my parents. My mom says he's a slimeball. But Dad says there must be some charm about him, because every time he sees him he has a different girlfriend."

When school was out, Mom was waiting for me. "You're going to have to help this afternoon," Mom said as I clicked my seat belt. "I'll be upstairs. Marshall said he'd help too. If he has any questions, you can show him what to do."

I didn't have to ask Mom why she was staying upstairs, and I knew that she knew I understood. When we got home, I put on my black suit and purple tie and put the worm in my pocket.

Marshall was setting up folding chairs in the back of the chapel. Dad was in the front, arranging flowers. Several new pots had arrived. "You want me to get some more stands from the garage?" I asked.

"That would be great," Dad answered as he wrestled with some stray ivy. "I could use four, at least."

I went out the front entrance and around the building to the hearse garage. It was still a couple of hours before the funeral. The parking lot was empty except for Mr. Stiller's black Corvette, and it was off in the side lot instead of in its place as part of the funeral procession behind the hearse. No one else knew the Stillers were there.

I went inside the garage and found the stands under an old tarp. They were dusty, so I wiped them down with an old rag. Then a loud thump shook the outside wall.

I heard a voice: "Stop, Dad—"

Then a louder whump, this time as if something had been thrown against the wall. I ran out the door and eased my way around the side of the garage.

Chuck whimpered. "Please, Dad, please—"

Mr. Stiller had his son pinned against the wall. He forced Chuck's arm behind his back in an unnatural twist.

"Please don't break it again, Dad. Please."

"You make me sick," Mr. Stiller said. The words slurred out of his mouth, thick and slow. He let go and Chuck dropped to the pavement.

Mr. Stiller picked up the flat bottle at his feet and took a drink. Then he pitched the bottle hard into the field beyond the parking lot.

The odd odor I'd smelled on Stan Stiller the night before was whiskey.

Chuck rolled over and made a weak attempt to crawl away. Mr. Stiller slammed his shoe into the small of Chuck's back. "Get up, you stupid little pig!"

Chuck curled in pain, but didn't make a sound.

I ran to the front of the garage just in time to throw up. I wiped my face and mouth with my handkerchief. Another spasm, and I leaned over, hands on my knees, and threw up again. Water ran from my eyes and a couple of drops hit my freshly polished shoes. I wiped my mouth again. My hands trembled.

Now I knew why Stiller was dirty and mean and always coming to school bruised up. I thought about how many times I'd been so angry I wanted to beat him up, to make him scared of me. But I couldn't imagine anything worse than being scared of your own father.

I'd never prayed before, and didn't think I knew how. But it must be something people are born with, like an instinct. *Oh God,* I cried inside, *I'm so sorry now for being mad at Chuck, for not trying to understand him. Please help him, God. Please.*

I tiptoed back to the other side of the garage.

"Why couldn't you be like your brother?" Mr. Stiller's voice was colder—and deader—than any corpse we'd ever had in the Paramount. "You're too much like your mother. I wish you'd died with her. How come Derek had to be the one to die?"

Chuck rose up on shaky legs. Mr. Stiller slapped him hard across the face, knocking him into the wall again. Chuck's body went limp and began to slide, but before he totally collapsed his father pulled him up by his hair.

"Look at you." Mr. Stiller spit into Chuck's face. "You can't even keep from wettin' on yourself." He expelled his disgust in long, drunken breaths: "I hate you."

He let go, and Chuck tumbled into a crumpled, beaten heap, lying in his own urine.

I didn't know what to do. I had to do something, but what? Mr. Stiller was bigger and stronger than me, not to mention drunk to the point of being senseless, so drunk that he couldn't tell he was killing his own son.

I had never been so scared—or felt so helpless—in all my life.

But I was more afraid for Chuck.

Chuck moaned, and Mr. Stiller reached for him again. I pulled out the radio. My hands were shaking like crazy.

"Dad," I whispered, "call 911."

No answer. Were the batteries dead? I tried again. Still no answer. Mr. Stiller had Chuck back on his feet. More than anything, I wanted my father. He would know what to do.

I wanted my mother. Her face flashed through my mind. Chuck had probably wanted his mom too, many times. But his mother had been dead for years. The thought made my churning stomach hurt even worse.

I wanted to take back all the mean things I'd said to Mom about moving, about the Paramount, and especially about Kelsey.

I felt so weak, confused, and powerless.

Oh God, I prayed again, *don't let Chuck die.*

I didn't know what else to do.

Dear God, please help Chuck.

I put the radio back in my pocket, and someone said, *Help him.*

Help him? How? What could I do? Mr. Stiller had Chuck up against the wall again. Chuck didn't care anymore, didn't even sniffle. My blood was pumping so hard the ends of my fingers and toes throbbed.

The woodpile!

Help him! Help him, Kevin!

I grabbed a length of two-by-four from the mound of scrap lumber beside the garage. I ran around to the back and, with my best home run swing, whopped Mr. Stiller in the back as hard as I could.

Mr. Stiller fell forward, and he loosened his grip on Chuck. Chuck fell to the pavement again, and from the corner of my eye I could see him trying to use his good arm to scoot away.

"This is none of your business!" Mr. Stiller yelled. "None of your business!"

He lunged toward me.

Swing again! Swing now!

I swung the board again, hard as I could, and hit him on his left side, knocking him off balance. But I lost my footing too. Disoriented, I dropped the board and teetered the wrong way, toward the garage.

Mr. Stiller sprang like a panther and pinned me to the wall. He pressed his forearm across my neck and leaned into my face. His gold chains jingled, and the whiskey smell on his breath made me want to vomit again.

"Get away from me." His growl sounded strangely like his son's. "Get away from me or Daddy will be burying you next."

I heard a loud crack, and Mr. Stiller's eyes rounded. He staggered back.

Dad was behind him, holding the same piece of wood I'd used on Mr. Stiller. I heard sirens.

Mr. Stiller swung at Dad, but Dad was quicker and decked him with an undercut. Mr. Stiller rolled on the ground, cursing Dad, and swearing he'd come back with a gun and shoot every one of us.

And there was Mom, kneeling beside Chuck. She raised his shoulders and cradled him in her arms. She took off her scarf and wiped his face.

"He won't hurt you anymore," I heard Mom whisper. She rocked him back and forth, as if she were rocking a baby. "Everything's going to be all right now."

Stiller's good arm went up around her neck, and she smoothed his hair with her hand. She looked at Dad. Her own hair was disheveled. Her mascara had run off her eyelashes and down her face, leaving black stripes on her cheeks. Her bottom lip quivered.

"Is Kevin hurt?" she mouthed.

Dad shook his head no.

Drizzle began to fall from the darkening sky.

Two police officers ran over. One called for an ambulance and some backup. All the energy drained out of my legs. I grabbed Dad's arm to stay on my feet.

"Hang on, Kev," Dad said.

Mom held thirteen-year-old Chuck Stiller in her lap. The asphalt had torn her hose to shreds, and her green silk dress was blackened and snagged.

Stiller clung to Mom for dear life. She kept him in a tight embrace near her heart and whispered something in his ear. I didn't understand what she said.

But as I watched her comfort Chuck, I felt like I was beginning to understand my mother.

My legs weakened again. Dad knew it before I did, because he put his arm around me to keep me steady before I had a chance to fall. I could feel his arm tighten as he held me up. I'd forgotten the familiar feeling of his skin against mine, and how he always smelled like Dial soap. It was the safest, most comforting smell in the world.

Thank you, God, I prayed inside again. *Thank you for my mom and dad. Thank you for listening. Thank you for helping me when I was most afraid.*

The drizzle turned into a steady rain.

Dad put his other arm around me, and I let him hug me—something I hadn't done in a long time. Before I could stop it, a tear mixed with the rain on my face and dripped off my chin. "I love you so much, Dad."

"I know, Son."

I couldn't stand it any longer. I buried my face in his shoulder. "I don't think I tell you enough," I sobbed into his shirt. "I don't think I appreciate you enough."

Dad hugged me tighter, and for a moment, he didn't say anything. Then his shoulders began to tremble. Soon he was crying too. Crying like that day I saw him in the chapel—the day I learned about Kelsey.

"I love you too, Son," he whispered, his voice shaky. "I don't tell you that enough, either."

Chapter Nineteen

I couldn't sleep that night. I thrashed around in the bed and kept thinking of all the awful things Chuck's dad had said. I could still see the pain on Chuck's face when his dad said, "I hate you." I didn't know which one would hurt more, the words or the punches. How could a father say or do those things to his own son?

I stayed home from school the rest of the week. Mom rented movies to keep me occupied, and Marshall brought me Hunk-O-Choklit bars every day. Marcy said I was her hero, and she knew those chin-ups would pay off someday.

Dani called me every day after school and came to see me that Friday night, along with her dad. While she helped me catch up on homework, President Carter sat in the kitchen with Mom and Dad and talked with them for a long time. When Dani and her dad were ready to leave, Dad asked President Carter to give a prayer. We had never had any kind of prayer as a family before. But as I knelt between my parents and listened to the words of President Carter's prayer, I thought about how God had blessed me with good parents, something I'd never considered until we moved to the Paramount. As they left, Dani hugged me good-bye—in front of her dad, without even acting embarrassed. And President Carter shook Dad's hand, telling him to call when he felt ready to come back, whatever that meant.

I spent a lot of time in the back lot that week. I'd go out early, before daylight, since I didn't sleep too well. At night I'd stay out past the ten o'clock news, just staring out at the mysterious shadows that shivered in the evening breeze. By the weekend I'd recorded so many minute details that I had to start a new notebook—Volume X.

But I couldn't hide out at home forever. Mrs. Goldwyn talked to my parents every day

I was absent to make sure I was coming back to school. I didn't want to, but I knew I had to. Finals were coming up. So on Monday I gritted my teeth and went back to Armadillo Middle for the last ten days of school.

The other students left me alone. No one asked what had happened; no one pestered me to tell the story. Dani stayed with me as much as she could. The teachers treated me as usual, but a few times I heard fragments of their conversations in the halls: "Did you hear about Stan Stiller?" "He got what he deserved." "That poor kid. It's a shame he had to suffer so."

Chuck Stiller didn't come back to school. I didn't want to talk about what had happened, so I didn't ask anyone about Chuck's absence.

At the end of the week, Mrs. Goldwyn called me to her office.

She motioned to a chair upholstered in thick green velvet. "Sit down. We need to talk."

I sank into the seat cushion. I felt very small.

"Chuck's uncle from Michigan—his mother's brother—and his wife took Chuck home with them a couple of days after Mr. Stiller was arrested. Chuck's going to live with them. I don't know what's going to happen to Stan Stiller, but frankly, I don't care. My only concern was that Chuck would have a safe place to go. I met his uncle and aunt when they came to get his records. They'll take good care of him.

"I know you and Chuck didn't get along, Kevin. You can't be principal and not pick up on things like that. But I want to tell you that I'm proud of you for controlling your temper around him. I know at times that must have been a real challenge."

I couldn't stop the hot tears—they spilled out automatically. It was so aggravating. I don't think I ever cried as much as I did that year. I hated to cry, especially in front of other people. Mrs. Goldwyn scooted a chair beside me and rested her hand on my arm.

"It's OK, Kevin. I know it's been tough."

"It's not that," I said, wiping my eyes with my fist. "It just was so horrible—his dad talking to him like that, beating him like that. I don't understand it."

"I don't understand it either. But I hate to think what might have happened if you hadn't been there and hadn't been willing to help him."

On the wall behind Mrs. Goldwyn's desk was an old photo of a young Cletus McCulley in his military fatigues. I could see his straight, white teeth. It was a black-and-white photo, but you could tell by the gray shade of his eyes that in real life they were sky blue. I reached into my pocket and pulled out the purple worm.

"Your grandpa liked to fish, didn't he?"

Mrs. Goldwyn seemed puzzled by the sudden shift in conversation. "After he retired, he and my grandmother fished almost every day," she said. "He once said his goal was to fish every lake in Arkansas. But as he got older and Grandmother got sicker, he did well to fish here in Sherman County. Why?"

"I wish I could have known him," I said, and stuffed the worm back in my pocket. But even as the words came out, I realized they were wrong. I did know Cletus McCulley. I couldn't explain how, but somewhere inside me I knew I did.

I excused myself and went back to class.

Chapter Twenty

When Mom picked me up from school that afternoon, she had this big, weird, I've-got-a-secret grin.

"How was school?" she asked.

"OK."

She strummed her fingers on the steering wheel. "Weather's supposed to be good this weekend. No rain, warm, plenty of sun."

"That's nice."

"It would be a great weekend to do some stuff outdoors, wouldn't it?" She was trying not to tell me something, but I hadn't slept well since the episode with Stiller's dad, and didn't feel like getting excited over anything but a few hours of good sleep.

When we got to the Paramount, Mom pulled the S-10 around back. A big yellow pickup truck—diesel, I could tell by the sound of the engine—was idling in the parking lot. Hitched to the truck was a bright red trailer, and on top of the trailer was a massive, mossy-green Bass-Catcher float boat.

I jumped out of the S-10 and ran over to get a better look. The diesel truck was a fine piece of work, but the boat . . .

Two padded seats, beverage holders at both ends, neat little compartments tucked around the edges to hold all kinds of gadgets—the boat was a dream. There were at least ten different fishing poles stashed in the bottom. And two tackle boxes. One was a beat-up old metal box; the other was shiny new plastic with clear amber sides.

Mom grabbed my arm and pulled me toward the home. "You'll have time to look at that later. You need to hurry."

We went in through the guest kitchen entrance and up the stairs to the apartment. I could hear Dad talking to someone.

When we reached the top of the stairs, Mom shoved me through the door. "We're back!" she shouted. "Sorry we took so long,

Mr. Conrad. Traffic was a little heavy this afternoon. It always is on Fridays."

"Not to worry, Mrs. Kirk," Herb Conrad said as he reached out to shake my hand. His eyes crinkled. "The fish won't start bitin' good 'til dusk anyway."

Chapter Twenty-One

Halfway to Herb Conrad's fishing cabin, we stopped at an old brick building that served as a combination roadside grocery store and bait shop. The dilapidated sign out front said *Mom and Pop's General Store,* but the paint was so faded it was almost unreadable. Mr. Conrad gave me ten dollars and told me to go in and buy some snacks.

"Spend the whole ten. And make sure you get me a Dr Pepper," he said, shaking his finger. "I don't drink nothin' but Dr Pepper. Don't try to fool me with none of that generic slop, either."

The sodas were in a big case that looked like a freezer. I lifted the lid and got out four bottles. I grabbed some packaged peanut butter crackers, beef jerky, peanuts, and some candy bars that were on sale three for a dollar. It all totaled to $9.02, so I threw in several pieces of nickel bubble gum to make up the difference.

Then we were back on the road again. I couldn't believe I was sitting in Herb Conrad's truck, eating his peanut butter crackers, and going to his cabin for an overnight fishing trip. Just as amazing was the secret Mom told me while we packed.

When Mr. Conrad said the fish wouldn't start biting until dusk, Mom dragged me to my room. "Come on, Kevin! Do you want to go fishing or not?"

"Well, yeah," I answered. "I'm just surprised, I guess. What do I need to bring?"

Mr. Conrad scratched his chin. "Old clothes, a change of underwear, a toothbrush. I've got the gear. Oh, and wear old shoes, not your good ones."

I ran to my room. Mom followed. I dug through my pile of grubby work clothes and found some old camouflage pants and T-shirts. Mom got the duffle bag from the closet and the shoes I mow the lawn in.

"Do you know why Mr. Conrad is here?" Mom asked as we stuffed the clothes in the bag.

"To take me fishing. I can't wait."

Mom stopped and took my hands in hers. Her eyes were big with excitement. "Kevin, Mr. Conrad is here because your father called him. We've both been worried about you, being depressed and all that. He knew this was something you'd wanted to do for a long time."

"I didn't know I was that obvious."

Mom laughed, and pointed to the copy of *A Beginner's Guide to Fishing in Arkansas* in the bag.

"Don't you see what this means, Kevin? Mr. Conrad is a member of the Church. Your father called him on his own, without prompting from me."

"So you think he's having a change of heart about God and the Church?"

Mom crossed her fingers and held them up under her chin. "Oh honey, I hope so. I'm praying for that now. You pray too, OK?" Then she put her hand on my cheek. "I love you, Kevin."

"I love you too, Mom."

"Well," she said, "we'd better hurry."

I put Volume X, two mechanical pencils, and my binoculars into the bag and zipped it shut. Mom and I walked together to the bedroom door. But before I could open it, I had to tell her something too.

"I'm sorry for the mean things I said to you about Kelsey, Mom."

She smiled.

"And I'm proud of you," I added.

"Thank you, Kevin." Her eyes glistened. "I'm proud of you, too."

Chapter Twenty-Two

Herb Conrad's fishing cabin was really the walk-out basement of a house that sat on the bank of Morpheus Lake, about a ninety-minute drive from Armadillo. He had a permanent rental agreement with a wealthy businessman in Little Rock who vacationed on the top floor during the summer. "Nice extra income for me and the missus," Mr. Conrad said.

When we arrived, Mrs. Conrad was there. It took a full day of dusting, sweeping, mopping, fresh sheets on the beds, and a couple of cans of disinfectant spray to chase the musty smells of winter away, she said. She was a big-boned woman who would have been anyone's first pick when choosing sides for a neighborhood football game. She had a pretty good grip, too. My hand tingled for several minutes after she shook it.

Mrs. Conrad sent us off to the river with a Playmate cooler full of bacon sandwiches, potato salad in individual serving bowls, and two big hunks of homemade pecan pie wrapped in foil. Mr. Conrad and I didn't catch any fish that night, but we sure ate good. And he taught me about the different kinds of rods, reels, and bait, plus some rules of basic boat safety.

That night I had my own small room to sleep in. The room was an afterthought—plain, with nothing in it but a hide-a-bed and a floor lamp for light. Mr. Conrad and his wife slept in the one real bedroom. Both rooms opened up to the combination den and kitchen.

It took me a long time to go to sleep that night. It was a little chilly, so I burrowed down under the clean sheets. Mr. and Mrs. Conrad snored really loud—so loud it sounded like he had backed his diesel truck up to my door and left it running.

I fell asleep sometime, though, because Mr. Conrad banged on the door about five A.M. "Hop up, Kevin. Let's go!"

Normally, I would have dropped back on the pillow at that hour, but Mrs. Conrad was frying sausage, and the smell was fantastic. I jumped up and dressed quickly.

Mr. Conrad sat in front of a big plate of sausage, eggs, and gravy. A ton of biscuits were piled up on a platter beside him. Mrs. Conrad bustled around the tiny kitchen, moving jars from the cabinets to the table.

"Come on, Kevin. Your biscuits are getting cold."

My plate was piled up as high as Mr. Conrad's. "This is a lot of food. I don't think I can eat it all."

"You'd better eat it, Boy," Mr. Conrad said. "Imogene ain't no woman who can stand seeing good food go to waste. You can tell that by lookin' at her."

"Herbert!" Mrs. Conrad's laugh was loud and boisterous. "By the looks of that gut, you don't waste much yourself. I fixed enough so you boys could take sausage biscuits to eat on the lake. So don't feel bad, Kevin, if you can't eat it all."

I was glad she said that, because by the time I finished eating I was afraid I'd sink the boat. But

I figured if Mr. Conrad could eat two platefuls and not be worried, the boat must be pretty sturdy.

We pushed off from the bank just as the sun filtered through the tops of the trees. For a long time, we just sat in the boat and floated with the current. We didn't talk. It was nice just to be outside where everything was still and to feel the sun gradually warm my shirt.

Finally, Mr. Conrad said, "Do you still have that bait I gave you?"

I pulled it out of my right pocket. "I carry it with me every day."

I could tell that pleased him. He took it and rolled it between his fingers. "You left it in your pocket once, didn't you?" he said. "And your mom accidentally washed and dried it."

"How'd you know?"

"I do it all the time. Makes Imogene so mad. Especially when one falls out in the dryer and she reaches in for the clothes and there's a squirmy feelin' thing in there." He chuckled. "That Imogene, she can be a real hellcat when she's mad."

Mr. Conrad picked up his rod, checked the artificial bait on the end, and then cast it. The bait made a graceful arc across the bright spring sky, then dropped down until it disappeared beneath the water's surface. The water rolled in quiet, glassy ripples from one side of the lake to the other. The air smelled like the blue-green algae that separated the water from the shore.

Mr. Conrad offered me a can of soda. I took a Dr Pepper, since that's all there was in the cooler. I popped the top and fizz sprayed my face, making me flinch. Mr. Conrad laughed. I stuck my tongue out and licked off some of the spray. It was sticky and cold, but tasty on what was becoming a hot day. I wiped the rest of it off with the back of my hand.

Mr. Conrad fingered through the pile of rods at the bottom of the boat. He picked out a black graphite beauty and handed it to me. It looked new compared to the rest of the bunch.

"This is for you, Kevin," he said. "To keep."

"But I—"

"Now listen, Boy. No arguments. The missus and I got this for you, and the tackle box, too." He nodded to the plastic one with the clear amber lid. "Think of it as my way of thankin' your father for doin' Cletus right at his funeral. Your father's a good man. I hope he comes back to church someday."

"Thank you, Mr. Conrad," I said quietly. How did he know about Dad? Then I thought maybe he'd believe me if I told him about Cletus McCulley. For a second, I wanted to. But I chickened out.

"Now what should we bait Kevin's hook with?" Mr. Conrad rummaged around in my new tackle box. "This spinner looks good. Perfect for catching largemouth bass."

"You mean *Micropterus salmoides.* That's the scientific name."

Mr. Conrad snorted. "If you're so good at readin' about fish, then show me how good you are at catchin' 'em."

And all at once the dream came back to me. The dream I'd had about fishing with Cletus McCulley. The dream that didn't seem like a dream at all. This lake, Morpheus Lake, was the same as the lake in my dream. The boat was the same, the rod and reel, the tackle box, the fizzy soda, the heat of the sun, and the smell of the algae.

"Mr. Conrad," I asked, my heart racing, "do you miss fishing with Cletus?"

He never looked up from tying the spinner. "Every day, Kevin. Every single day of my life. Cletus lived as Christlike a life as anybody on earth could. That man was like a brother to me."

The question just blurted out of my mouth. But I had to know. If anyone knew, it had to be Cletus McCulley's best fishing buddy. "Can a dead man go fishing?"

Mr. Conrad finished tying the spinner, then looked at me with a grandfather-knows-best kind of smile.

"I believe he can, Kevin," he said. His eyes searched deep within mine, as if he had just found a kindred spirit. "After all, there's more to life than what we see."

Chapter Twenty-Three

I was glad when the last bell rang on the last day of school—and the last day of seventh grade at Armadillo Middle. But I still had to go back one more time, for Awards Night. I wore my skunk tie, since it was Dani's favorite. She looked pretty in her black-and-white-striped dress with the yellow sweater. A few of the teachers asked us if we dressed that way on purpose, because we looked like a matched set. Dani blushed and said that it wasn't unusual for best friends to dress alike.

The faculty gave out several awards, probably because they didn't want anyone to feel left out. Dani got a U.S. History award, a writing award, a citizenship medal, and a certificate for perfect attendance. I got an award for having the highest grade point average in the seventh grade, which I hadn't expected at all. Mom, Dad, Marcy, and Marshall were my cheering section. When I went up on stage they hollered and Marshall whistled really loud. I should have been embarrassed, but I liked it.

When we got home that night, Marcy had a surprise for me in the guest kitchen. She opened the freezer and pulled out a big ice cream cake. She apologized for the decoration—an ugly mallard duck done in brown and green gel. The only other cake at the Dairy Queen big enough had Cinderella on it. I told her the duck was fine, since all that mattered to me was whether or not the cake tasted good. But I did think the writing on the cake was strange:

CONGRATULATIONS
UNCLE KEVIN

"Oh, Marcy," Mom slapped her hands over her mouth. She grabbed Marcy's arms. "Are you—?"

Marcy grinned. Then she and Mom hopped up and down. All Mom could say was, "Oh, Marcy! Oh, Marcy!"

Dad slapped Marshall on the back. "Good job, Marshall! We're all so happy for you!"

Happy for what? I looked at the cake again. CONGRATULATIONS UNCLE KEVIN. The only thing strange was the uncle part. Why would Marcy do that?

In the instant I thought the question, I knew the answer. Mom and Marcy were still bouncing, so I grabbed Marcy's arm to make her stop. "Marcy, are you gonna have a baby?"

Marcy laughed and wrapped her arms around me. "Uncle Kevin, I thought you'd be the first one to figure it out!"

We sat down to eat the cake before it melted. Dad said I should get the first piece, so I had him cut the chunk off the side that said UNCLE KEVIN. We stayed up late that night in the guest kitchen, eating cake and making plans for the new baby. By the time we went upstairs to bed and Marcy and Marshall went back to their apartment, it was after midnight.

Before I opened my eyes the next day, I could tell by the heat of the sun on my face that it was after eight. I got up and ate a bowl of cereal and drank a glass of juice. Mom and Dad were still asleep, so I dressed, put the worm in my pocket, and left a note for them on the table:

> Mom and Dad,
> Riding my bike into town. Be back in a couple of hours.
> Love, Kev

We'd lived in Armadillo for almost a year, and this was the first chance I'd had to ride my bike. It was the old one. I still hadn't bought a new one. We'd been so busy I hadn't had time to ride anyway. This was my first time out alone, too, but I wasn't worried about getting lost. By now I was pretty familiar with the town. After all, it wasn't that big.

I came upon a yard sale a short distance down the road. I parked my bike and wandered around, trying to mingle in with the old people who were out hunting for bargains. I dug through a box of books, hoping to find a cheap field guide for birdwatchers. Instead I found a worn-out Book of Mormon.

What did Mom and Dad read in this book that made them want to join the Church?

I flipped through the pages. Lots of verses underlined, lots of words scribbled in the margins.

I tried to guess what Cletus McCulley's Book of Mormon must have looked like and felt certain it would have been even more well-worn. I decided then and there if Cletus McCulley had read it, so would I. Dad had a denim-covered Bible on the bookshelf in the den that he got when he was in college. I figured he wouldn't mind if I borrowed it too.

I carried the book with me as I scanned over the rest of the junk. While going through a box of baseball cards, I accidentally knocked a rusted toy truck onto the ground. I bent down to pick it up and found an old fishing pole under the table.

A woman sat on the front porch, holding a pencil, notepad, calculator, and a cigar box full of money. I carried the book and pole to her. "How much for these?"

"Five dollars." Then she noticed the book. "Wait a minute. Where did you find that? I hadn't planned to sell that."

"I'd like to have it," I said. "A friend of mine is Mormon." I figured she didn't have to know he was a dead friend.

Her face softened. "Keep it. My son is serving a mission right now. Who knows, maybe you will too."

I dug down in my pockets. I had two dollars, thirteen cents, and a ball of lint. I hesitated for a second, then thought, well, all she can do is tell me no. "Would you take two dollars and thirteen cents for the pole?"

A mother pushing twins in a stroller walked up and gave her a handful of crumpled-up bills. The woman nodded to the armload of baby clothes the mother carried. "This will be fine. You go ahead. You've got your arms full."

She smoothed the wrinkled money out in her lap. I was afraid she'd forgotten about me, so I cleared my throat. "How about two," she said, never looking up from counting her money. "I don't like dealing with odd amounts of change."

I handed over the cash. I stuck the book in my pouch, strapped the pole to my bike, and took off again. But instead of riding into town,

I decided to ride away, out in the country. I turned off a side road, crossed a bridge that spanned the edge of a small lake, and then turned onto a narrow gravel road. It was quiet and the sun was heating things up. But the trees were full and everything smelled green and moist.

Up ahead, the road ended at a clearing. A good place to see deer in the evening, I thought. But as I got closer I could see rows of gray and white stones off to the right. It was a cemetery. I parked my bike and walked around.

I remembered Dad saying once that graves are sometimes plotted to face the east, so I figured I must have been at the west end of the cemetery, since I was facing the backs of the stones. As I walked to the other end, I looked back at the markers and found some of them dated back to the early 1800s. A few of the oldest stones were so weathered that the engravings smoothed out into nothingness.

One large, newer stone was made from deep, gray granite, polished to such a shine that the sun's reflection made it stand out like a beacon in the center of the field. There was something carved on the back that I couldn't make out from where I stood. As I moved closer, the engraving became clear:

DEATH IS A FISHERMAN—
AND WE THE FISHES BE.

I shivered from my neck to my heels, despite the ninety-degree heat. The name engraved below the epitaph was MCCULLEY.

I stepped around to the front of the stone. The name CLETUS DARNELL was etched on the left. GLENDA SUE was on the right. And in the center were two wedding rings, entwined with ribbon and held in the beak of a dove, with the words underneath TOGETHER FOREVER.

I pulled the worm from my pocket. It was warm and squishy from the heat, but still held its shape.

I ran back to my bike for the two-dollar fishing pole. I carried it back to the grave and sat down on the ground. I wanted to say something, but what do you say to a tombstone? So I just sat there for a long time.

Finally, I nestled the handle of the fishing pole into the artificial flowers in front of the grave. I fixed it so it stood at an angle, just as if it were being used to fish. I let the line out and stuck the hook in the ground. I stepped back to admire the result. It looked pretty neat. I figured Cletus McCulley would like it.

I thought about putting the worm on the hook. But I figured Cletus McCulley would want me to keep that.

"Thanks, Mr. McCulley," I said out loud. "Thanks for everything."

A soft rustle came from within the thick honeysuckle vines growing up the trees along the edge of the cemetery. A long, brown, scaly snout poked through the leaves, then a pair of beady black eyes followed by two tall, pointy ears.

Armadillos may be ugly, but they are interesting. This one's nose scoured the ground in search of a six-legged lunch. He must have been nearsighted, because he acted like I wasn't even there. Or maybe he couldn't see me because, like a fish, his eyes were stuck on the sides of his head.

I got back on my bike and headed home. Granddad and Grandma were coming in tonight from Florida. They were going to spend a whole month with us. There would be lots of stuff to get ready. We'd have to move my birdbaths again, and I wanted to organize all the family history papers Grandma gave me into a special notebook, so she would know I hadn't forgotten them—or her. Mom and Dad would most likely have something they needed me to do too.

I flew down the gravel road, into the soft late-morning wind. I turned onto the side road that led to the highway, and as I approached the bridge I slowed down and looked out across the water.

An old man and his wife were fishing. He yanked his line out of the water. A huge fish was at the other end. He hauled it into the boat. The fish flopped around, struggling to get free of the hook. The woman clapped her hands as the old man removed the hook from the fish's mouth. As he put the fish in the cooler, his wife leaned over and whispered something in his ear. She pointed at the bridge where I stood, and the old man called out, "Hello, Son!"

I waved and shouted good morning. The wife fluttered her handkerchief in the air. The old man waved his hat, revealing crew-cut hair whiter than the wisps of clouds overhead and eyes bluer than the sky's reflection on the sweet summer water.

About the Author

For Patricia Wiles, one of the most fun things about being a mom was reading books to—and with—her three children: Ami, Jessica, and Aaron. Now that her children are grown, she enjoys writing for readers of all ages and interests. She was a public radio commentator for five years, has had poetry published in regional publications, and her essays have appeared in *Writer's Digest* and *The Writer.* She is currently a weekly columnist for her hometown newspaper and a member of the National Society of Newspaper Columnists. She is also a member of the Society of Children's Book Writers and Illustrators. Patricia lives in Madisonville, Kentucky, with her husband and best friend, Tim—and a spoiled-rotten, bob-tailed cat named Bandit. You can write to her in care of Covenant Communications, P.O. Box 416, American Fork, Utah 84003-0416, or email her via Covenant at info@covenant-lds.com.